"Sara?" he said. This was late at work, pure and simple. Why else would we have ended up at the very same high school?

"My mom is in Japan," I said stupidly. As if that explained *anything*. "I moved here to live with my dad for the year."

Josh was shaking his head back and forth, back and forth, looking confused and bewildered.

"Sara . . . I can't believe it." He took a step forward and squeezed my hand.

My heart leaped. "I wanted to call and tell you I was moving here," I said. "But I didn't have your address. . . ."

"Yeah, I know. . . ." As quickly as he'd grabbed my hand just a moment ago, he now let it drop to my side.

"Josh?"

He was looking over my head, his blue eyes intent. "Raleigh," he said.

I spun around. Raleigh was standing right behind me. And she was beaming at Josh. "Hi, babe!" she chirped happily. "Great game."

"Thanks." Josh stepped away from me as if I'd just announced that I'd recently been exposed to the Ebola virus.

I watched in horror as Raleigh threw herself into Josh's outstretched arms. "Hi, Sara," Raleigh greeted me after she finally separated herself from Josh. "Did you meet my boyfriend?"

What We Did Last Summer

Elizabeth Craft

BANTAM BOOKS
NEW YORK • TORONTO • LONDON • SYDNEY • AUCKLAND

RL 6, age 12 and up

WHAT WE DID LAST SUMMER

A Bantam Book / January 1999

*Produced by 17th Street Productions,
a division of Daniel Weiss Associates, Inc.
33 West 17th Street
New York, NY 10011.
Cover photography by Michael Segal.*

ISBN: 0-553-49255-1

Published simultaneously in the United States and Canada

*Bantam Books are published by Bantam Books, a division of Bantam
Doubleday Dell Publishing Group, Inc. Its trademark, consisting of the
words "Bantam Books" and the portrayal of a rooster, is Registered in
U.S. Patent and Trademark Office and in other countries. Marca
Registrada. Bantam Books, 1540 Broadway, New York, New York 10036.*

PRINTED IN THE UNITED STATES OF AMERICA

OPM   0 9 8 7 6 5 4 3 2 1

For Mom and Dad

Prologue

I WISHED FOR the tenth time that morning that I'd planted an explosive device in the engine of the large yellow school bus that was going to whisk Josh out of my life (at least, out of the state of Maine and my immediate range) for the foreseeable future. If that bus didn't run for some reason, I would've had extra minutes, hours, days in his arms.

Unfortunately I was a law-abiding citizen who wouldn't do something as ill-advised as destroying an entire school bus. That being the case, I clung to Josh, my arms tight around his neck, as if sheer force of will could keep us together forever.

"This summer has been awesome," Josh said. "You're an amazing girl, Sara."

"Thanks," I croaked, staring into the intense blue of Josh's eyes. How was I going to live without that blaze of color in my life? "You're pretty great yourself," I managed to whisper.

"Oh, Sara." Josh's arms gripped me even more tightly, and I felt his strong hands move up and down my back.

I almost wished that last night hadn't been so wonderful. Josh and I had snuck out of our cabins as usual and paddled across Lake Vermilion to our favorite little island. He'd surprised me with a midnight picnic of strawberries and sparkling cider (I still didn't know where he'd found the fake champagne). We fed each other strawberries and made wishes on the dozens of shooting stars that streaked across the velvet sky. Slightly cliché? Yes. Romantic? Most definitely.

Josh and I had stayed up most of the night, talking and laughing. And there had been a lot of kissing. And whispering. By the time we'd paddled back to Camp Quisiana, the sun was rising over the pine trees. Never had I been so sorry to see the start of a new day.

Now I had to face up to the fact that Josh was just minutes from boarding that horrible yellow bus. This morning Josh and I and all the other junior counselors had gathered at the dining hall and made an extra-special breakfast—pancakes, waffles, bacon, and sausage. We'd even pushed all the tables outside so that the kids could eat in the sun. All morning I'd tried to pretend that this was just another meal—but I couldn't live in my fantasy world any longer. This was it. This was good-bye . . . for now, at least.

"Josh." I buried my face against his chest, not

caring two you-know-whats whether or not Gunnie, the camp director, was glaring at me from her post at the head picnic table. There was a time for restraint and there was a time for making out in public. This morning—the last that Josh and I would spend together for a long time—was without question a time for the latter.

"I mean it," Josh whispered against my hair. "You're one in a million. Two million. A billion."

I nodded mutely, longing for those three magic words to come from his lips. "So are you, Josh. . . . I love you." Oh, no. Had those words really just slipped out of *my* mouth? *I love you.* Yes, mental instant rewind had proved me right.

Josh cupped my chin in his hand and tilted my face up to his. "Me too," he whispered.

I smiled. Okay, so Josh hadn't come right out and uttered the I-love-you phrase. But I'd read enough teen magazines to know that guys weren't exactly pros at declaring their undying love. I didn't need to hear those words—simply knowing that Josh felt the same way about me that I felt about him filled my whole soul with sort of a warm glow.

"And we'll see each other soon," I said. "Maybe I can spend Thanksgiving with my dad." My father had recently moved to a tiny Florida town, which Josh had assured me wasn't too far from the coastal town where he went to high school.

Behind us I heard the blare of the bus horn. My stomach sank into my toes as I glanced over my shoulder. The first bus of the day was ready to depart—campers and counselors were leaving in shifts, depending on the time of their various flights. I wasn't leaving until late this afternoon, when Mom would arrive to drive me back to Portland. The bus driver stuck his head out of the window. He looked cranky—and extremely impatient.

"Let's go, lovebirds!" he yelled. "Time doesn't stand still just because you two aren't ready to go."

"Be right there!" Josh called back. He turned to me. "Looks like we've had a pretty large audience."

I looked around—Josh was right. Dozens of pairs of eyes stared at us from their seats on the bus, and still more campers were gazing at Josh and me from their spots at the picnic tables. I felt my face turn a deep crimson.

"I gotta go," Josh said.

I nodded silently and watched him take a single step toward the bus. Then I suddenly shrieked, "Ohmigosh! Josh! Wait!"

He turned. "What is it?"

"Addresses! Phone numbers!" Man, this was totally typical of me. Dealing with practicalities isn't exactly my forte. "We don't even know how to get in touch with each other!"

Josh dropped his backpack and banged his fist against his forehead. "How could we have forgotten?" he asked. Then he shook his head. "Never mind—I *know* how we forgot."

He didn't have to expand on *that* statement. There had been dozens of times when I'd been on the verge of asking Josh for his vital statistics. But

4

somehow my address requests were always lost in a fresh, all-consuming kiss.

He pulled out a crumpled receipt and a black laundry marker from his backpack. "Okay, give me your address."

"160 Little Hill Road," I began. "Portland, Ma—"

"We're leaving *now*, Nelson," one of the counselors yelled from the bus. "And I mean *now!*"

"Hurry," Josh urged. "Give me the rest."

"Portland, Maine, 04101," I finished quickly. "And my number is 207-555-6215."

Josh stuck the cap back onto the marker and stuffed the receipt into the back pocket of his faded Levi's. "I'll miss you," he said.

"I'll miss you too," I answered, a huge lump forming in my throat.

Josh leaned forward, brushed his lips lightly against mine, and gave my hand one last warm squeeze. "We'll see each other soon. I'm sure of it."

And then he turned and sprinted to the bus, where the driver was scowling at us from behind the large, rather dirty windshield. I watched as Josh's perfectly sculpted shoulders disappeared into the vehicle, then craned my neck so that I could see him move swiftly down the narrow aisle. The driver honked twice, then threw the bus into reverse. And they were gone.

It wasn't until the bus had vanished down the long dirt road that I realized I hadn't gotten Josh's address and phone number. All I knew was that he lived in Florida, in a town called Mason's Cove. Or was it Mecca Beach? No, wait. The name of the town was Cove's Corner. Or not. Oops.

I sighed deeply but shrugged it off. Josh would call me tonight from the Sunshine State—or at the very latest tomorrow. I would write down his stats in a safe place . . . and then I would write him the longest, funniest, most romantic letter he'd ever received. After that it would be only a matter of time before we made concrete plans to see each other again.

Dear Josh,

Hi! I miss you so much. There, I got that very important statement out of the way. Now I can continue this letter with . . . what? I don't know exactly what I want to say. I can't wait to get your first letter. I'm so anxious to communicate with you that I decided just to go ahead and start writing you letters whenever I feel like it. Then I can put them all together and mail them to you as soon as I get your address.

This summer was so amazing. Before I met you, I never thought I could be serious about a guy. Usually I date someone for a month and then wish they would more or less get lost. But with you . . . I don't know. It's like I'll never discover all there is to know about you. I could talk to you for hours and hours and not be bored for even one second. Incredible, isn't it?

Okay, I'm getting ultrasappy, so I'm going to end this now. Maybe I won't even send it. All I know is that I'm dying to talk to you. Did you copy my phone number down wrong?

Love,
Sara

P.S. The state of Maine isn't the same without you in it.

One

"**M**OM, THIS IS going to be my *senior* year in high school!" I exclaimed. "You can't actually expect me to switch schools *one week* before the semester starts."

"I've been offered the opportunity of a lifetime. I just can't say no." My mom sighed softly and leaned forward on the sofa so that she could give my knee a maternal pat. "I'm sorry this is such short notice, but the university didn't know whether or not there was going to be enough money for my research grant until two days ago."

I was lying on the faded green couch that lined one wall of our living room, where I'd been pouting for the last hour. As day after day passed without the arrival of a letter from Josh, I'd found myself sinking into a serious funk.

Okay, so it had only been a week and a half since camp had ended. But I'd expected Josh to write me the minute he'd arrived home. I knew that the mail was probably just taking an extra-long time or that Josh's letter had even gotten lost somehow. But it was still pure torture waiting to hear from him.

Plus the fact that Josh hadn't called me yet had to mean that in our rushed good-bye, he'd copied down my phone number wrong. And since my mom had a different last name from me, there was no way he'd be able to find me through 411.

In fact, I was sure that at this very moment Josh was placing a call to Gunnie to beg my vitals from her. I knew that *I* had a call in to our camp director. Since I couldn't remember the name of Josh's town, I'd had no luck finding his phone number through information. (Note to self: Pay attention next time love of my life tells me the name of his hometown.)

I'd had a moment of pure elation when I found Josh's E-mail address on the Internet, but after I'd sent him numerous messages without getting a response, I realized I must have had the wrong Josh Nelson. Just my luck.

But as of ten minutes ago I'd discovered that an empty mailbox wasn't my only problem. I now had a totally valid reason for this particular mope session.

Japan. My mother was moving to Japan. And I was expected to drop my entire life—including the thousands of activities I'd planned for my all-important senior year—and pick up somewhere new. Not to mention the fact that I'd now be ridiculously far away from Josh.

I flung one arm over my eyes and sighed so loudly that my chocolate Labrador retriever, Georgie, trotted across the hardwood floor and plopped her head onto my stomach. "Go ahead and ruin my life," I said to my mother in my best martyr voice. "It's no big deal. Just one little life among billions."

"Sara . . ." She sounded tired. I knew that tone—it was the one designed to make me feel like the worst daughter in the world. As usual, my mother succeeded. I felt lousy.

Okay, so my mom had spent, like, years preparing for this moment. She had toiled over huge tomes about the history of Japan in Portland's public library almost every night for the past three years, doing research for her Ph.D. thesis. But as Mom had told me on more occasions than I could count, one can only do so much obscure research in Maine. Mom needed access to a lot more material if she was ever going to finish the thesis she had nicknamed "The Monster."

And now the University of Maine was offering her a full-ride scholarship to go study at the University of Tokyo for a year. But still, there was the matter of my *own* life. I had plans. Big ones. And *none* of them involved moving to Tokyo.

"I know, I know," I said. "You've worked your butt off for this moment. All the sacrifices, all the time, all the migraine headaches are about to pay off. And you simply can't let the opportunity pass you by."

"Exactly." She sounded happy now. Happy and excited. "This year is going to be a real-life dream come true."

A dream come true for you, I thought. Meanwhile my own destiny was about to be changed forever. My killer senior year at Thomas Jefferson High and any hopes for continuing my relationship with Josh had just flown out the window—and all the way to Japan.

Talk about the mother (excuse the bad pun) of all bad days. Today I had somehow gotten the notion that volunteering to be a hair model in order to obtain a free cut and shampoo from Sandy at the Ambience Salon was a bright idea and had been given the worst haircut of my entire life (which is saying quite a lot). And of course, there was no way I could forget that today marked day ten of me not receiving a letter from Josh. So much for the glorious, waning days of summer. Life was a big, black hole.

And now my mother was wearing her I-know-it's-hard-to-be-a-kid-but-that's-just-too-bad expression.

"I'll live with the Golds," I said suddenly. "I can sleep on Maggie's floor." That wouldn't be so bad. A nine-month-long slumber party with my best friend had definite fun potential. There was simply no way I was going to relocate to Japan right now. No way.

"Absolutely not," my mom said. "You and Maggie together night and day spells nothing but trouble with a capital *T*."

"Come on, Mom. That's ancient history." Apparently Maggie and I were *never* going to live down the time we'd decided to spray a gigantic shaving-cream peace sign onto the football field. Or the night we borrowed—I stress *borrowed*—Mr. Gold's car so that we could drive to New York for a Hole concert.

She shook her head. "I've already talked to your dad. You're going to Florida for the year." She paused. "And that's that."

"Florida!" I shrieked. "Florida!" *Florida, Florida, Florida. Josh. Florida.* My head felt as if it were going to explode as the word rolled over and over in my mind.

True, the state was basically a million miles from my house, friends, and school. But Florida was also the home of Josh Nelson. The possibilities played out in my mind as if I were watching a cheesy Danielle Steel TV movie. I smiled. This day was improving at a rapid rate. Next to me Georgie barked. I guess she sensed my abrupt shift in mood.

"Where did you think I was going to send you?" Mom asked. "Algeria?"

"Of course not." My heart was beating so fast that I felt as if I were in the middle of racing the Iditarod. She had no idea that she'd just dropped the biggest gift of my life into my lap. And I wasn't about to tell her—parents had a way of bursting bubbles. Especially bubbles that happened to be six feet two, blond, blue eyed, and male. "I just didn't think you'd send me to Florida . . . that's all."

"Your dad has finally established some roots. I think you two spending this time together will be wonderful for both of you." Mom flipped her shoulder-length dark hair over one shoulder and looked wistfully into the distance—the way she always did anytime the subject of my well-meaning but flaky father came up.

Most people think of dads as gray-haired men who come home at five-thirty carrying a briefcase in one hand and flowers for their wife in the other. Okay, maybe fathers aren't like that in reality. But a dad is at least expected to live in one place, have a job, and take his kid to the occasional baseball game.

My own father is a sculptor who, until recently, believed that a Winnebago, license plate number LPJ8683, was enough of a permanent address for anyone. Usually he showed up in Portland three or four times a year, parking his Winnie on the street in front of our house. He would hang around for a couple of weeks, teach some art classes, sell some pots, and then head back out onto the open road. He had lived in almost every state you could think of and had just bought the house in Florida over the summer. Settling down in one place had been a major step for him.

"Maybe you're right," I said. "Dad and I haven't really had a chance to *bond* since I was, like, ten years old." I knew the father-daughter bonding issue was huge with my mom. "And I can see if he's serious about the whole settling-down-and-becoming-a-real-adult thing."

Mom grinned. "It's settled, then. We're both starting new lives exactly one week from today." Suddenly a shadow fell across her face. "There's only one problem."

Uh-oh. "What's that?" I asked breathlessly.

"I'm going to miss you like crazy." Mom held out her arms.

"I'll miss you too," I said, collapsing against her. And I would. But missing my mother seemed relatively unimportant compared to reuniting with my love. Right now the only thing I cared about was getting to Florida and finding Josh.

One week. *Just hang on for one week, Josh. I'll find you . . . and then we can be together forever.*

"I can't believe you're leaving. I can*not* believe it." Maggie had repeated those same two sentences approximately fifteen hundred times since first hearing the news of my departure. But now that moving day was approaching, there were tears in her voice. Maggie's bright green eyes were sad, and even her curly red hair seemed a bit droopy.

I stuck yet another wig on my head. This one was long, dark, and bangless. Since receiving the worst haircut of my life, I'd been obsessed with the idea of buying a wig. We'd spent the last forty-five minutes in Sunny Wigs and Beauty Supply, where I'd tried on over a dozen heads of hair.

"Maggie, we've been over this." I didn't want to admit it, but I was on the verge of a major bawl session myself.

Maggie pulled the brunette wig off my head and replaced it with a shoulder-length auburn *Friends* 'do. "I just can't believe you're leaving," she said again.

Emotional good-byes are not my thing. I hadn't even cried the day I said good-bye to Josh. At least, I hadn't shed any tears in his presence. Once I was back home and alone, I'd crawled into bed, pulled the covers over my head, and let loose with about a bucket of tears. Then I'd dried my eyes and partied with my friends at a welcome-home bash.

"You have *tons* of friends," I pointed out, tugging off the fake hair. "Besides, with me out of the picture you're a shoo-in for homecoming queen." I plucked a curly blond wig from the counter and plopped it onto Maggie's head.

"Gee, thanks for the vote of confidence," she answered dryly.

"Hey, that's what I'm here for," I said breezily.

"Correction. That's what you *were* here for." Maggie handed me a dark blond wig. I liked the style—shoulder length with short Cleopatra bangs.

The girl was *not* playing fair. "Mags, you know I'm never more than a phone call or plane ticket away."

She nodded slowly, then smiled. "Oh, well, at least when I come to visit, I'll get a fabulous tan." During the years of our friendship I'd pretty much indoctrinated Maggie with my no-negativity philosophy. Like me, she never stayed down for long.

I stared at myself in the mirror, half satisfied

16

with my reflection. I could live with this hair until my own golden locks grew to their former, glorious length. I was, however, suddenly keenly aware of the fact that if I were ever to get a bad cut in Florida, Maggie wouldn't be there to hold my hand (or my hair). It was a horrible thought. *Stay positive,* I ordered myself.

"Do you think Josh will like me in this wig?" I asked, anxious to turn the conversation away from our impending best-friend separation.

Maggie shook her head. "You're not going to still be wearing the wig by the time you get to Florida, Sara."

I shrugged. "You never know. I might decide I like fake hair better than the real stuff." I paused, frowning at myself in the mirror. "I mean, *look* at me. My head resembles a worn-out mop."

Maggie rolled her eyes. "Okay. I recognize misplaced anxiety when I see it."

"What's that supposed to mean?" I asked, turning away from the mirror.

"You're worried about you and Josh, aren't you?" She tapped her foot, waiting for me to respond.

I said nothing. I'm not too into the wishy-washy girl-bonding stuff. And I hate to admit self-doubt. It's simply not my style.

"Come on, Connelly," Maggie continued. "I know you. You're worried because you haven't gotten a letter from him."

It wasn't a question. It was a statement. "Yes," I

admitted. There was no need to expand. I had, after all, been obsessing over the vacant mailbox and silent telephone every waking moment. And I'd come up with a million reasons why Josh hadn't written to me yet. The most plausible scenario was that Josh had lost my phone number and address somewhere between Maine and Florida—we all know that scraps of paper have a way of disappearing into the ether.

Maggie waved her hand dismissively. "You know he wants to talk to you—he's simply experiencing a little technical difficulty."

"I know," I said. "But now he'll never be able to get in touch with me! Even if he found my address and wrote to me yesterday, I still won't get his letter before I leave!"

"I promised I'd check your mailbox every day once you're gone," Maggie reminded me. "And besides, if you guys are meant to be, it'll happen—you'll find each other."

I pulled the wig off my head dejectedly. "I'm not so sure about that anymore. I mean, just because we'll be in the same state doesn't mean it'll be any easier to track him down."

"But once you talk to your camp director, you'll definitely be able to get his address," Maggie pointed out. "Anyway, I know you—you always get what you want. You'll find Josh eventually."

"You're right," I said, feeling buoyed up again. "And when I finally do, he's going to be so thrilled to see me that he'll sweep me up in his arms and kiss me until I feel like I'm going to pass out." It was a daydream I'd had often during the past several days. It was what had kept me going.

"You got it." Maggie nodded vigorously.

I smiled at her, relief flooding through me. I bit back any doubts I had and focused instead on the positive fantasy of Josh's and my reunion.

"I love you, Mags." I had never said that to her before. Best friends usually didn't need to say that kind of stuff to each other. It was understood. But drastic times called for drastic measures, and this was definitely a drastic time.

"I love you too, Sara." Maggie took a step forward, and we hugged each other tightly. I felt as if I never wanted to let her go . . . but I had some business to take care of that simply couldn't wait.

Two

T HE SUN WAS a huge orange ball against a deep blue sky as I turned off the southeastern Florida highway exit marked Bay Beach on Saturday afternoon. According to the elaborate map my dad had faxed to me, his house was only about two miles from the off-ramp. I could already smell the ocean. The salt air was hot and dry, and I felt as if I had driven straight into paradise as I cruised along in my convertible, the sun beating down on my face and the wind blowing through my hair (I'd gotten a trim and, thank God, my hair looked normal again). Was it even legal to live in a state with weather this good?

It was too bad Mom couldn't make the whole trip with me. We'd driven down the coast together, then I'd dropped her off at the airport in Jacksonville, Florida. She was flying to Miami and then on to Japan. I already missed the way she nagged me incessantly about giving Georgie baths, cleaning my room, and remembering to turn off the coffeepot. But life went on . . . and mine was heading straight toward Josh and true romance.

"Aha!" I shouted to Georgie. On the side of the road was a large piece of pink poster board that read Sara! This Way! The board was attached to a wooden stake—by my dad, of course.

I kept driving, keeping my eyes peeled for more signs. Dad didn't disappoint. Every two hundred yards or so I saw another sign, each with a huge black arrow pointing down the road. I couldn't stop grinning. My father might not be the most reliable guy in the world, but he knew how to make a statement when he wanted to. This was the biggest welcome mat I'd ever seen.

And then I saw the small wooden sign: Hart Avenue. "This is it, Georgie," I informed my dog. As of this moment I was an official Florida resident. "This is the road that leads to our new life." Georgie obliged me with a loud bark and quick tail wag. Then she barked again.

"All right, already," I told her. "Yes, this is *also* the road that will hopefully lead me back to Josh Nelson, the most awesome guy ever created by the universe." I was so excited by the prospect of finding Josh that I had to remind myself he wasn't going to be standing on my dad's doorstep holding a bouquet of helium balloons.

I'd spent most of the drive down envisioning the moment Josh and I would meet again. Deep down I knew that there was a good chance I'd never see him again, but I had to stay positive—that was the only way this move would be bearable. And even though the idea was nothing short of insane, there was still a tiny part of me that hoped Josh *would* be waiting for me at Dad's.

I glanced from left to right as I drove toward my new home. The block was beautiful. Small, colorful houses lined both sides of the street, all with lawns big enough to have elaborate gardens planted out front. I passed the houses slowly, reading the addresses as I went. "We're close," I told Georgie. "Very, very close."

And then I saw the final sign: Welcome, Sara and Georgie! I honked three times as I turned into the gravel driveway. Almost instantly my dad popped out from behind some exotic-looking bush. I threw the car into park, switched off the engine, and banged open the door.

"Dad!" I let my key chain fall to the ground and ran into my dad's outstretched arms. As I covered the short distance between us I noted that he'd trimmed his formerly butt-length hair to a fairly respectable shoulder length. He'd even shaved his mountain-man beard into a neat goatee.

He swept me up into a huge bear hug. "You don't have to call me Dad," he reminded me. "We're equals. You can call me Mark."

Okay, so the man still fell under the category of aging hippie. At least he was wearing an actual shirt rather than the horse blanket-turned-poncho he usually sported. And there was a real *house* looming behind him. After years of hard work and wandering, Dad had finally started to earn enough money to do the things that most people did in their late twenties—he now owned a home, had health insurance, and actually filed income taxes. "Thanks, but I prefer the more traditional *Dad,*" I said, laughing.

He shrugged. "Whatever makes you happy, sweetie."

Behind me Georgie bounded out of the Oldsmobile. She headed for my dad, barking happily. I watched as my father's face lit up—he loved Georgie almost as much as I did. For the next couple of minutes the man-dog reunion was full tilt. There aren't many people who don't mind getting dog saliva all over their face, but my father is definitely one of them.

Yep. Easygoing, laid-back, and all smiles. Dad might be adhering to more of society's rules these days, but he obviously hadn't changed too much. And I was glad that I was going to be able to get to know him better. Cross-country trips during school vacations and sporadic phone calls just weren't the same as day-to-day living. Dad and I were going to have a whole new dynamic.

But right now it wasn't the father-daughter stuff that was burning a hole in my brain. I had Josh on my mind in a major way. I couldn't wait to begin the search. And somehow, some way, I intended to start the Josh hunt tonight. First stop: Dad's white pages. Second stop: Put in yet another call to Gunnie to try to find out the name of Josh's town. And finally I planned to try the E-mail route once more.

If my first three fact-finding missions failed, I had a more elaborate plan. Going to the library to look through phone books had been Maggie's brilliant, last-minute brainstorm. The idea was so simple, yet so perfect. I would simply look through every Florida phone book in the library until I found the one with Josh's phone number.

The plan had only one hitch. Nelson wasn't exactly the most unique surname in America, and I had no idea what Josh's dad's first name was. I could wind up dialing a hundred different Nelson families looking for Josh. But my love knew no bounds, and blind dialing was a task I was all too willing to perform.

"Who's up for a veggie burger?" Dad asked. "I've got the grill fired up out back."

I rolled my eyes. I'm as politically correct as the next daughter of ultra-aware parents, but I like to eat meat now and then. Especially the kind of meat that's served on a bun and slathered with ketchup, mustard, and dill pickles. "Can we at least barbecue some chicken?" I asked.

He shrugged. "No problem, hon. I'll go over to Tim's and snag some poultry from his parents' freezer."

"Tim? Who's Tim?"

My father grinned. "Tim's my new assistant.

He's a very talented young man. . . . I think you're going to like him."

Uh-oh. My dad had a certain tone in his voice. A tone that I'd heard Mrs. Gold use whenever she tried to convince Maggie to go on a blind date with some guy whose father worked with Mr. Gold at Greater Portland Insurance. But this couldn't be true. My dad was a freewheeling, peace-loving, enlightened hippie. He knew better than to butt his way into his daughter's private life. I decided to give the man who was half responsible for my presence on earth the benefit of the doubt and assume that I'd been mistaken about the matchmaker's voice.

"You have an assistant?" I asked. "That's great!" My dad is an amazing sculptor—his work has been shown in some of the best galleries in the United States. But his sense of business . . . well, it sucks. Mom and I had always thought he would benefit from hiring someone to take care of the banal stuff that goes along with making an actual living.

"Tim is more than an assistant," Dad said. "He's a gifted young sculptor who's going to make a real impression on the art world someday."

"The artist thing is nice," I said. "But can this Tim guy keep your books for you?"

"Yep. He's also witty, your age, and single." Dad ticked off Tim's attributes as if he were selling a cheap pair of earrings on the Home Shopping Network.

"Gee, is he house-trained?" I asked sarcastically.

Dad retrieved my enormous duffel bag from the

backseat of my car and hoisted it onto his left shoulder. "Tim has already promised me that he'll show you around the area," he continued proudly. "And I offered to spring for dinner and a movie for the two of you."

"Dad!" I was truly groaning now. What had happened to my ultracool dad? Apparently his brain had been spirited away by aliens and replaced with the mind of Mike Brady from *The Brady Bunch*. I mean, even if I didn't already have my own plans in the romance department—which I one hundred percent *did* have—I certainly didn't want my father prearranging a love life for me.

He headed toward the house, Georgie following close behind. "Whatever you say, hon. I just want to make sure that the transition to sunny Florida isn't too traumatic for you."

"I'll be fine," I assured him. *In fact, I'll be superb as soon as I get my hands—and lips—attached to Josh.*

I suddenly realized that I'd stopped in my tracks. My thoughts were wandering over and around Josh, blocking out everything else, even the ability to put one foot in front of the other. I was halfway up the narrow brick path that led to my dad's front porch before I even took in where I was. My jaw practically dropped to the ground. The place looked more like a gingerbread cottage than a real-life house.

The house was two stories high and painted a lilac color usually reserved for Easter eggs. Each window was trimmed in mint green, as was the long wooden porch that stretched the length of the house. Clearly Floridians were a bit more whimsical than those of us who hibernated for ten months a year in Portland. The front door was the pièce de résistance. Someone—very possibly my dad—had painted a six-foot mermaid, complete with a long curling tail and waves lapping at her feet, on the door. The minimural was interesting but not exactly my taste.

"Hurry up!" Dad called from somewhere within the house. "You can get unpacked while I get started on dinner."

"Coming!" I yelled.

Dad appeared at the door and poked his head outside. "And I want to hear all about your mom. It sounds like she's as fabulous as ever."

I made a concerted effort not to sigh. My dad had been pining after my mom ever since the divorce. He hadn't dated a woman for more than a month in over ten years. The poor guy still had a broken heart. Hmmm . . . maybe there was another reason that fate brought me to Florida at this particular juncture of my life. If my father felt free to try to find me dates, then maybe I should do the same for him.

"What's that look on your face?" Dad asked.

"What look?" I asked innocently, smiling my perfect-daughter smile.

Then I jogged down the rest of the path, my heart beating fast. I was about to have my first official meal in my official new house in my official new town. Yep. My official new life was beginning. Which meant one very exciting thing—with any luck, there was a chance that Josh could soon become my official boyfriend.

The sweet, heavy smell of the Florida morning forced my eyes open at eight o'clock on Sunday morning. Sunlight poured through the window of my new bedroom, and I could hear the sound of my dad's pottery wheel spinning in his downstairs studio. I nudged Georgie, who was still fast asleep at the foot of my bed. She opened her eyes and thumped her tail happily. Unlike me, Georgie is a morning person—well, a morning dog.

I'd fallen in love with my room the moment I'd laid eyes on it the night before. It was big, with hardwood floors and yellow walls.

"This is our first morning in Florida, Georgie," I said softly. Sooner or later I was going to have to stop counting firsts; the list could be endless: First time I brushed my teeth, first breakfast, first walk to the beach, first shower.

"Honey?" Dad shouted from downstairs. "Are you up?"

"I'm up!" I called back. "There better be some Raisin Bran down there!"

I slipped out of bed and walked past the full-length mirror that stood in the corner of the room. I had a horrible case of bed head. Unfortunately my new wig was already useless—apparently I needed to spend more than $29.95 if I was planning to wear the fake hair on a regular basis. But I wasn't about to attempt to drag a comb through my mass of tangles until I had at least one cup of coffee in my system. Otherwise people—or dogs—could get hurt.

The sound of Dad's pottery wheel got louder as I padded downstairs in a pair of bunny slippers. Luckily I also detected the distinct scent of caramel-nut coffee—my absolute favorite. Dad might not have been around all that much when I was going through those so-called difficult adolescent years, but at least he'd been paying attention.

"Coffee. Give me coffee," I groaned as I shuffled into the kitchen.

"Let me guess," a deep voice said. "You like it light and sweet."

I gasped. Sitting at the large pine table was a guy about my age. He grinned. "Sara, I presume?"

"Uh, yeah," I responded as smoothly as I could, considering the fact that I was wearing a purple flannel bathrobe and bunny slippers. "And who might you be?"

My voice instantly went into flirtation mode. Yes, I admit that I can't be in a room with a cute male my age and not give off what Maggie had dubbed the flirt vibe. And yeah, the guy *was* cute. He had short dark hair and full red lips. His eyes were so brown, they were almost black. I mean, my passionate love for Josh hadn't made me blind to healthy male specimens or anything.

"I'm Tim Kaplan," he responded easily, as if

running into bathrobe-clad girls in random kitchens was an everyday occurrence in his life.

Then it clicked. Tim Kaplan—Boy Who Would Be Sara's First Floridian Date. He was also the guy who was going to help my dad become a bona fide yuppie. "So," I said. "You're the talented young assistant who's going to make sure my dad remembers to pay his bills on time."

Tim laughed. "Before I started working for him, the electricity had already been turned off twice."

"And he probably hadn't been paid for, like, the last dozen pieces he sold," I added.

"You got it." Tim stood up and walked toward the coffeepot. "Do you take it with half-and-half or skim?" he asked as he poured me a large, inviting mug of caramel nut.

"I'm a half-and-half girl. Life is short."

"Sugar?" he asked.

I nodded, then watched as Tim scooped out three spoonfuls of sugar from the vaguely dinosaur-shaped sugar bowl I'd made for my father in third grade.

"Do you also like bungee jumping, fast motor-cycle rides, and hang gliding?" Tim asked, handing me the mug.

I took a sip of coffee as I glanced at Tim. "I said life was short. I didn't say I had a death wish."

"What about scuba diving?" Tim asked. "I haven't lost a customer yet."

"How did the conversation turn from half-and-half to scuba diving?" I asked.

"I'm a scuba-diving instructor." Tim placed the

empty coffeepot in the sink, then picked up a worn sponge and ran it along the tiled countertop. "I'd be more than happy to teach you—free of charge, of course."

I considered Tim's offer as I watched him continue to tidy the kitchen in a methodical, mindless manner. The guy's familiarity with my dad's kitchen was a little unnerving. I mean, I was the daughter here. I was supposed to be the one who felt at home, not like a houseguest. I didn't like the idea of being a stranger in a strange town. I wanted to belong, just as I had in Portland. And making a friend would be a good place to start.

"I'd love to learn," I told Tim. "Just name the day."

"We'll go after school one afternoon. I'll check my schedule with your dad and let you know."

I nodded. Less than twenty-four hours in town, and I already had plans. Not bad for a seventeen-year-old girl with bed head. I hoped Mom had as easy a time adjusting to life in Japan—I couldn't wait for the call I was expecting from her tonight. Who knew? Maybe by the time I talked to Mom, I would have found Josh and started to really feel at home. Okay, maybe that was being a bit too optimistic. But no one ever said a girl couldn't dare to dream. . . .

By the time I sat down to dinner on Sunday night, my initial love affair with Florida had taken a slight beating. I'd had no success locating Josh in

32

the phone book, I'd discovered there wasn't a decent place to shop within fifty miles, and I'd fried myself at the beach. Clearly I was going to have to enter phase two of my plan—the library.

I'd tried calling Maggie three times that afternoon, but each time Mrs. Gold had informed me that my best friend was out with "the gang." Apparently my absence hadn't done any damage to the Portland social scene. Everyone seemed to be getting along just fine without me.

"Why are there three place settings?" I asked my dad, who was busy smothering our pasta and tomato sauce in parmesan cheese.

"I'll be your distinguished guest this evening." Tim emerged from my father's studio, his hair matted with patches of clay.

"Oh." I didn't want to be rude, but I was getting kind of sick of having the master assistant around. He hadn't been away from our house for more than five minutes since the second I'd arrived in Bay Beach. "Don't you ever go home?"

"Sara!" My father turned away from the huge bowl of pasta. "What's your problem?"

"Nothing . . . sorry." What was wrong with me? Poor Tim had been nothing but nice to me. Apparently my stress over searching for Josh was having a negative impact on my ability to be civil. I sat down at the table and forced a smile for Tim.

Dad plunked the bowl of pasta onto the middle of the table and slipped into one of the chairs. "Tim made a gorgeous vase today. You should take a look at it."

I nodded absently. My mind was still on the search. "Yeah, definitely."

Tim whistled. "With that kind of enthusiasm in my corner, I might as well have my own show at MOMA."

I looked down at my silverware and didn't say anything. I was *not* in the mood to be teased.

"Who wants garlic bread?" Dad asked. "I got this loaf from an organic farmer up in Coral Gables."

I held out my plate. "Thanks."

Tim was staring at me, trying to get me to respond. Well, he could stare all he wanted. "Don't worry about your lack of interest," he said. "I mean, it's not everyone who can appreciate great art. You're probably more into watching soaps and reading *Teen People*."

Okay, that was it. I lifted my head and stared back at him. "For your information, I don't watch television unless forced to do so by a close friend. And I don't read *People*. Teen or otherwise."

Tim laughed—a fast, easy laugh that I'd noticed this morning. "Relax, Sara. I'm just teasing."

I held my angry gaze for a moment, but after taking in his playful brown eyes, I couldn't help cracking a smile. He was right—I *was* totally over-reacting. Still, I didn't have to admit to it. "I know," I told him. "So am I."

"Uh-huh," Tim responded, clearly amused. "Right."

My dad stuck two pieces of garlic bread on my

plate. "Are you nervous about tomorrow, honey?"

No, Dad. Not at all. First day at a new school isn't any cause for alarm. "Of course not," I said. "I don't get nervous."

All right, so I'd confided to my mom when she'd called that there were some enormous butterflies in my stomach because of my upcoming first day in a new school. But Tim didn't need to know that. Some information is better kept to oneself.

Tim raised one dark eyebrow. "I'd be happy to give you a lift to Glendale and show you around. It can be a pretty overwhelming place."

I plunged a fork into my pasta and shook my head vigorously. I was not going to let Tim take pity on me. "I'm an adventurer. I like to do things on my own."

He nodded, his eyes sparkling. "Whatever you say . . . as long as you don't wimp out on the scuba-diving session."

"Don't you worry about that. I'll be there." One small nightmare—the one I'd had last night in which I'd drowned next to a school of sharks—wasn't going to keep me from delving into the beautiful world of the deep sea.

"Great!" Dad said in that irritating voice he seemed to have picked up since reading a copy of *Fathers and Daughters: The Importance of Boosting Self-Esteem.* "Sara isn't nervous, and my two favorite teenagers are going to embark on an underwater odyssey. Life couldn't be better."

So Dad was laying on the corny life-is-perfect

35

attitude a bit thick. But he did have a point. It suddenly felt comforting to have Tim around, even if he did get on my nerves a bit. After all, he had managed to lighten my mood tonight. And I *was* looking forward to learning how to scuba dive. . . .

Still, life *could* be better—a lot better. And I was sure it would be if I could just locate Josh. Then life would be just about perfect.

Sara's Official Oprah-Style Gratitude Journal

I figure new places call for new routines, so I'm going to take Oprah Winfrey's advice and start my own Gratitude Journal. The idea is that if I write down five things every day that I'm grateful for, life will start to look different. I'll focus on the good stuff rather than the bad stuff. Usually I focus on the good stuff anyway. But I have to admit that being in a new town is a little more lonely and scary than I expected. So here goes . . .

I am grateful that my dad and I are going to spend time together.

I am grateful for the awesome weather.

I am grateful that my car didn't break down on the way to Florida.

I am grateful that Tim Kaplan (even if he is slightly annoying) seems willing to show me around and hang out.

Last but not least, I am grateful that Josh and I are now in the same state, even if I don't know exactly where he is just yet.

Three

"Sorry," I said, not for the first time that morning. I'd been banging into people right and left as I pushed my way aimlessly through yet another crowded Glendale corridor. Did I ever mention that I *hate* Mondays?

Glendale High isn't a school—it's a city. I'd never seen so many hallways and classrooms, not to mention students, packed under one roof. Even the administration office had been unusually packed. I'd had to wait almost ten minutes to talk to someone in charge. Now I held a map and a class schedule that Ms. Rodriguez had given to me after firing off a list of rules and regulations regarding dress and behavior. Basically I wasn't supposed to wear skirts that showed my underwear or obscene T-shirts, and under no circumstances was I to make out in the halls.

The girl I'd bumped into gave me a withering

glance and continued to storm her way down the hall. Evidently politeness wasn't a school rule. I pulled myself out of the stream of students and leaned against a bright purple locker. There was an unfamiliar shallowness to my breathing that I recognized immediately to be anxiety. I also noted that my palms were sweaty, and I more or less wished that the floor would open up and swallow me whole, new clogs and all.

I couldn't believe that just a few days ago I'd been under the illusion that I'd simply move to Florida, look up Josh in the phone book, and fall into a life full of love, fun, and friendship. So far I'd managed to get a bad sunburn, make myself sick on clam dip, and stay up all night worrying about my first day at a brand-new school. And as far as Josh went, I was realizing just how big a state Florida was.

A quick stop at the school library—luckily I'd bumped right into it—had shown that there were at least two hundred phone books. Looking up the name Nelson and copying down all the possible phone numbers could take weeks. And I could just imagine my dad's reaction to the phone bill padded with the cost of calling several hundred Nelsons all over the state. At least Gunnie was due to arrive back from her postcamp hiatus any day now. She had the power to give me Josh's phone number and hometown in an instant.

"Lost?" A petite girl with shiny dark hair and the kind of smile usually reserved for the National

Cheerleading Championship was beaming at me. She looked a little perkier than the kind of girl I usually hung out with, but hey, I needed friends wherever I could find them.

"Lost is a total understatement," I said. "I've been wandering for what feels like an eternity."

"You're new," she said in a voice loaded with sympathy. I felt instantly guilty for having mentally derided the girl solely based on the fact that she had one of those cute button noses.

"Yeah. I just moved down here from Maine." I smiled in what I hoped was a friendly manner.

"Well, welcome to Florida! I'm Raleigh Stockton." She stuck out her hand, which I shook awkwardly.

"Sara Connelly," I told her. "And I'm in desperate need of some kind soul to take mercy on me."

"Say no more." Raleigh took the schedule from my hand and studied it for a moment. "You're in the wrong building, for starters. Mr. Maughn's classroom is in Kingman House."

"Oh." So much for me ever making it to first-period calculus. I had no idea there even *was* another building, much less how to find it.

"I'll take you there," Raleigh offered.

 felt a rush of pure gratitude. "You don't have to," I said meekly. "I mean, you must have to get to class yourself."

She shrugged. "Everyone around here knows me. I'll just tell Ms. Martin that I was showing around a new kid."

Groan. I was a new kid—the most dreaded label

in high schools all across America. "Thanks," I said.

Raleigh glided through the hallway, and I followed docilely behind. Was this how Georgie felt when she yapped at my heels?

"So, are you coming to the football game on Friday?" she asked.

"Uh . . . I don't know." I'd always gone to the games in Portland, but there I'd been an integral part of the social scene. And I hadn't actually watched the field. Football games were always just more opportunities to party.

"You should," Raleigh advised. "It's a great way to meet people." She gave me a huge smile; clearly she had dealt with so-called new kids before. "I'd take you myself, but I have to cheer."

So she was a cheerleader. My perky radar had been right on target. "I'll, um, keep it in mind," I said. *Get a grip, Sara,* I told myself. *Try to find a personality somewhere within that fine self of yours.* No personality was forthcoming. "I mean, sure, I'll be there."

"Great!"

At the end of the hall she pushed open a huge red door. "Kingman Hall is down this path," she explained, charging ahead. "And the gym is down that way." She waved in the general direction of the enormous parking lot.

"Why is this school so huge?" I asked. "Bay Beach has a population of, like, fifty thousand."

Raleigh laughed. "Bay Beach only has fifty thousand people, but kids from all over go to

Glendale. Some students have to drive, like, forty miles just to get here."

Duh. The girl must think I was the biggest idiot on the planet. "Right, right . . ." How could I follow up such a dumb question? I was beginning to think I'd left the brain that had scored me a 1490 on the SAT back in Portland.

"The good news is that there are *tons* of cute guys around here," Raleigh said in a conspiratorial voice. "Someone as pretty as you are will have more dates than Jennifer Love Hewitt at a dirt-bike rally."

I laughed—my first genuine giggle of the day. First of all, I bask in compliments. Second, Raleigh had said something vaguely funny.

"I'm not sure I'm in the market for dates," I said. "I sort of have someone."

"Really?" Her eyes lit up. "I love to hear about other people's romances. I've been going out with the same guy since I was, like, eight."

This didn't surprise me. Girls like Raleigh always ended up with the boy next door. "Wow. That's a long time." His name was probably Biff or Skip or Ken.

"Yeah. So tell me about your man. Is he pining away for you back in Maine?"

"Uh, sort of." I hoped Josh was pining, at least.

"It's a bummer he's so far away," Raleigh said. "A boyfriend is pretty much useless if he doesn't go to school with you."

We agreed on that much. The mere thought of

attending the same high school as Josh was enough to make me turn into a babbling lunatic. I could see it now: I'd walk into Kingman Hall and into my calculus class only to find Josh standing in the middle of the room. But life didn't work that way.

"Well, I hope he's worth waiting for." Raleigh pointed to a small redbrick building on our left. "That's Kingman."

We both stopped. This was the moment—were either of us going to make an effort to become friends? Or were we going to silently acknowledge that we had nothing in common and let it go at that? "Thanks for the help," I said.

"You're welcome!" Raleigh responded enthusiastically. She appeared to be breathing a silent sigh of relief that I wasn't going to ask her over for a slumber party on Saturday night. "And good luck!"

Raleigh continued her bouncy walk down the path, leaving me alone in front of the building. The last bell had rung minutes ago. I now had to walk into a packed classroom, disturb whatever action was in progress, and have some cranky old math teacher announce my name. This hadn't been the best morning of my life. Then again, my hair didn't look half bad. And for now a good hair day would have to do.

I took a deep breath. "Glendale High, here I come."

That afternoon I lay sprawled on the couch with Georgie, watching *Oprah* and drowning in my own misery. Normally I never let myself get this down, but today I couldn't help it. Here I was, miles and miles away from home and with no real hope of ever finding Josh. Sure, I had my fantasies, but now I had to face facts—there was no way I would ever see Josh again . . . at least in the near future.

And of course on top of that I was at a new school with no friends. Not to mention that all my teachers had assigned a ridiculous amount of homework for the first week of classes. Life was beyond miserable.

"Hey, Sara." I looked up to see Tim standing in my living room, smiling.

I tried to smile back. "Hi," I mumbled.

Tim dropped down on the seat across from me. "You're not looking too good."

Great. Just what I needed—someone to reinforce my negative feelings. "Thanks a lot," I said sarcastically.

Tim laughed and shook his head. "That's not what I meant, Sara. You just seem pretty down."

I sighed and sat up straight. "Yeah, well, I had a long day."

"Mmm. First day of school wasn't a party for me either."

"At least this is your turf," I told him. "Being the new kid in school totally stinks."

"Is that self-pity I detect in your voice?" Tim's dark eyes glittered with amusement. "What happened to the girl who loves adventure?"

I let out a heavy sigh. "Listen, I am not in a good

mood," I warned him. "So if you want to tease me, now is *not* the time to do it."

Tim stood and threw his hands up in surrender. "Okay, okay, I'll give you your space." He reached into his backpack and pulled out a brown paper bag. "Actually, I figured you might be bumming and in need of a sugar fix, so I brought you this." He handed me the bag. "But don't worry, I fully understand the need to be alone. I have to go work for your dad now anyway."

"Oh." I peered into the bag, feeling bad for having snapped at him. The sack was filled with all sorts of Gummi candies—my absolute favorites. But how would Tim know that? As depressed as I was, I couldn't help smiling at the gesture.

I glanced up—Tim was walking out of the room. "Hey, Tim," I called after him.

Tim stopped in place and turned around. "Yes?"

"Thanks," I said, holding up the bag. "This was really sweet of you."

Tim shrugged. "That's what friends are for." Then he turned around again and headed for my father's studio.

I lay back down and bit into a sour-peach Gummi, feeling more relaxed than I had in hours.

At least I had one real friend in Florida.

"Did you go to a lot of football games in Portland?" Tim asked me Friday night. I had forgone my first scuba-diving lesson in favor of going to the football game together. Florida was enough of a shock to the system as it was—I didn't need to add underwater breathing to the bizarre nature of my current life just yet.

The game hadn't even started, and I was already bored. Tim and I had come to the game with Tim's best friend, Ed Pratt. As soon as Ed had spotted a group of freshman girls making goo-goo eyes at him, he'd gravitated toward them. Now Tim and I were left alone.

I shrugged. "Yeah, but it was different."

I'd always associated football with chilly fall nights, the smell of burning leaves, and the taste of hot chocolate. Tonight the temperature was around eighty degrees and the scent of honeysuckle permeated the bleachers. Maine had never seemed so far away.

"How so?" Tim asked. "Isn't football football?"

I shrugged. "I'm just used to knowing people, that's all." I wasn't exactly in the mood to go into details. Conjuring up images of me entertaining my huge circle of friends with my witty repartee and crazy antics was just plain depressing.

Sure, I'd find my place at Glendale eventually. But by that time it would be the end of senior year, and I'd probably end up at the prom with some dude whose idea of a good time was whale watching. Not that I thought there was something fundamentally wrong with whale watching. I simply wanted to regain my spot as homecoming queen hopeful and girl-most-likely-to-have-plans-any-given-night.

"Maybe not having tons of friends around will

be good for you," Tim commented. "It'll give you more time for self-reflection before you go off to college."

What was with him? Who needed self-reflection? I wanted fun. And romance. "Is that what *you* do all the time? Self-reflect?"

"Has anyone ever told you that you're quite prickly?" Tim asked. He took a sip of his smoothie and arched one dark eyebrow.

"No." I heard the pout in my voice, but I didn't care. Tim was the only person my age I'd conversed with in the past week. Therefore he was the unlucky recipient of the effects of my notorious bad temper.

He laughed. Jeez, the guy laughed *all* the time. He was so annoyingly comfortable with himself. *I* was the person who was supposed to be comfortable—I was popular and pretty and smart.

"Sara, can I ask you something?"

"Sure." I leaned back, closed my eyes, and tilted my face up toward the last remaining rays of sunlight, feeling as though all the energy had been drained out of me. "Shoot."

"Did you have a boyfriend back at home?"

My eyes popped open, and I bolted back up. Just the thought of Josh was enough to recharge my system. "Yes. Actually, a very serious boyfriend." The fact that we hadn't communicated in a month was just a minor detail.

"Aha. I see." Tim nodded. "So *that's* why you've been so cranky. You're missing your man."

It was beyond irritating that Tim could read my moods so easily. Was I that obvious? "I haven't been cranky," I protested.

Again Tim raised a single eyebrow. How did he do that anyway?

"Okay, so maybe I have been a *little* cranky."

"How big of you to admit it." Tim smiled, his eyes lighting up with that sparkle I'd noticed the other night. "Are you going to try to visit him? Or have you ended things because of the long distance?"

"Oh, Josh doesn't live in Maine," I explained. "He lives here. We met in camp."

Tim scrunched up his eyebrows, looking confused. "Here? You mean in Bay Beach?"

"I wish. The way my luck's been going, he probably lives at the other end of the state or something," I said, my frustration over the Josh search rising to the surface once again. "The thing is, he lost my phone number and address, and I never had his. The past couple of weeks have been pure hell, trying to find each other." Now that Tim had got me started on my favorite subject, there was no way I was going to stop. I was much too worked up. "You have to understand—Josh isn't just any guy."

"Oh."

"We're talking about love, the real thing, the whole nine yards."

Tim was quiet. Sitting there with him in the awkward silence that followed, I suddenly felt like a dork for having spilled out all my emotions to him.

Sure, he was easy enough to talk to, but I'd just met the guy. It wasn't like me to run at the mouth like that. And Tim's loss for words indicated to me that he wasn't that psyched with the turn the conversation had taken.

Embarrassed, I looked at him, but his eyes were cast down at his hands, as if he were seriously contemplating something. It was the first time I'd ever witnessed anything other than an easygoing expression on his face.

I nudged him. "Hey. Earth to Tim."

He glanced up, looking caught off guard. His cheeks tinged slightly pink. "Oh, sorry. I must've spaced there for a second."

"That's all right. I didn't mean to bore you."

"You didn't," he told me, shaking his head and looking more like the lighthearted Tim I was used to. "So, you said his name is Josh?"

"Yes." I couldn't hold back a giant smile as I conjured up an image of his gorgeous face in my mind. "Josh Nelson."

Tim's cheeks quickly changed from pink to white. What was going on with him anyway? I figured he must be sick or something. "Josh Nelson?" he repeated.

"Yep," I said, sighing blissfully. Even the sound of his name sent goose bumps up my arms.

At that moment there was a sudden burst of sound as a gaggle of cheerleaders emerged from the gym and ran out to the track around the football field.

"Give me a *G!*" the girls screamed in unison.

"*G!*" everyone in the stands echoed.

"Give me an *L!*" The cheerleaders began to organize themselves into a pyramid.

"*L!*" I wasn't surprised to see that Raleigh, my perky tour guide, was the girl heading for the top of the human pyramid. She was one of those petite girls born for chicken fights, piggyback rides, and gymnastics.

The chant continued at a deafening volume. In Maine, I would've been shouting at the top of my lungs. But here I was silent. It just didn't feel like my school.

I looked over at Tim and noticed that he didn't join in on any of the cheering either. He just sat there and stared out at the football field, still looking pale. I guessed he wasn't one for school spirit.

At last the noise died down. Tim tapped my arm. "Hey, um, Sara?"

"Yeah?"

He stared right into my eyes, looking rather serious for someone who was supposed to be having fun at a football game. "There's something I should—"

"Welcome, Gator fans!" A deep male voice boomed out over a loudspeaker and took my attention away from Tim. "Let's have a great Gator welcome for this year's starting lineup!"

I turned back to Tim. "What were you saying?"

He continued to stare at me for a long moment, then shook his head and looked away. "Never mind," he muttered. "I'll tell you later."

I shrugged and said, "Whatever you want." I focused back on the field and the emerging athletes.

At first the players were indistinguishable from one another. Put fifteen boys in white pants, a red shirt, pads, and a helmet, and it's difficult to identify any one of them. Then I found my eyes resting on number seventeen. There was something about his walk. . . .

I had seen that gait before—in my dreams, most recently. There had been trees and a deep blue lake and the smell of maple syrup. And Josh. I shook my head. I was *not* looking at Josh Nelson. It would be too much of a coincidence—not to mention a fantasy—that Josh and I would be at the same school. Besides, I knew for a fact that he didn't play football. Clearly longing and desire were driving me mad.

"Number eleven, Ben Wycliff," the announcer's voice cried. "Number fifteen, Art Preston."

I kept my eyes glued to number seventeen. But still, there was no way it could be—

"And number seventeen, Joshua Nelson!"

Joshua Nelson! He was here! My head pounded and my brain felt as if it were going to explode.

If I hadn't been able to feel every drop of blood in my body rush to my face, I would've thought that I'd died and gone to heaven.

"Sara!" Tim's voice buzzed in my ear. "Listen, Sara, there's something that—"

I shook my head excitedly. Whatever it was that Tim wanted to tell me would just have to wait. Josh was here! "Don't you understand?" I exclaimed. "That's him! That's Josh!"

"Yeah, but Sara—," Tim began.

"No buts!" I cut him off. "This is the best day of my life!" I closed my eyes for a moment, suddenly overcome by a wave of nausea from all the excitement.

"Now I think I'm going to throw up," I told Tim calmly. Then I stood up and ran for the bleacher stairs. I needed to find a bathroom. Pronto.

Four

GLENDALE HIGH WON the game. For two and a half torturous hours I'd roamed the stadium, counting down the moments until Josh would trot off the field. I had taken a moment to check in with Tim and let him know I hadn't completely ditched him—he was busy chatting with Ed, but when he spotted me, he tried to talk to me about something. There was way too much adrenaline coursing through my blood for me to sit still, so I told him whatever he wanted to discuss could wait until later. Then, for a full half hour, I'd hung around the bathroom, waiting for the corn dog I'd eaten to propel itself out of my system. Once it seemed that I wasn't going to barf, I'd spent another fifteen minutes applying, then reapplying, new coats of lipstick.

Now I was hovering at the edge of the field, watching the football players congratulate themselves with high fives and pats on the back. *Come on, Josh,* I urged silently. *I'm waiting for you! I'm here!*

I pressed one index finger lightly against my left wrist—my pulse was hammering away. Had I ever been this excited? Well, there had been the Christmas when I'd walked downstairs to find a shiny new bicycle waiting for me. But what was a blue ten-speed compared to the knowledge that my long-distance love wasn't long distance after all?

"Sara! There you are." It wasn't Josh who was heading toward me. It was Tim.

"Hi." I peeled my eyes away from the players and turned to him. "Sorry I haven't been much company for this game. But you understand—it's hard for me to stay in one place with Josh around and all."

"Right," Tim said, shifting his weight from one foot to the other. "Uh, I was thinking it might be a good idea for me to take you home."

"Home!" I exclaimed. "Are you kidding? I'm not leaving here without Josh!"

I didn't know what Tim's problem was, and at that moment I didn't care. I just wanted to run up and kiss Josh. I stepped back from Tim so that I could see the field clearly.

The football players started to leave the field en masse. For a moment I lost sight of number seventeen. "Sara?" Tim asked. "I really think—"

I waved away his comment. "There he is!" I whispered. "It's really him!"

Number seventeen had pulled off his helmet,

revealing the blond hair that I remembered so well. He was still several yards away, but I was certain it was Josh. I could almost taste his lips as I watched him walking closer and closer to the spot where Tim and I stood.

I staggered forward, vaguely hearing Tim call my name as I fell into the pack of football players, who were now just a couple of feet away.

And then he saw me. At first Josh's gaze skimmed over me, as if he were searching for someone in the stands. But a second later his gaze returned to my face. I saw the flash of recognition in his eyes.

"Josh!" I croaked out. I wasn't the speechless type. But at the moment, I felt my mouth opening and closing with no sound coming out. "Josh," I finally repeated in a hoarse whisper.

He was beautiful—even more beautiful than I'd remembered. The many photographs of Josh and me that I'd tacked to the bulletin board above my bed simply didn't do him justice. Man, he was hot.

"Sara?" His blue eyes shone as he looked at me. This was fate at work, pure and simple. Someone in the universe wanted Josh and me to be together— why else would we have ended up at the very same high school?

I nodded. How did one greet the love of her life at a moment like this? I swallowed several times, anticipating the feel of Josh's soft, firm lips against mine.

"My mom is in Japan," I said stupidly. As if that

explained why I was attending Glendale High's first football game of the season. As if that explained *anything*. "I moved here to live with my dad for the year."

Josh was shaking his head back and forth, back and forth, looking confused and bewildered. This wasn't exactly the open-armed, romantic reunion I'd hoped for. But I couldn't blame Josh for being shocked to see me. *I* was shocked, and I had known this encounter was imminent.

"Sara . . . I can't believe it." He took a step forward and reached for my hand.

My heart leaped. I saw love in his eyes—the same love I'd seen every day when we'd been together in Maine. I clasped his hand and intertwined my fingers with his. Warmth spread through my body.

I was dimly aware that we were surrounded by a dozen large football players and that Tim was standing nearby. But the lights, the stands, and the crowd all seemed to fall away as I stared into Josh's eyes.

"I wanted to call and tell you I was moving here," I said, the words rushing out of my mouth as quickly as I could speak. "But I didn't have your address. . . ." *And you never wrote to me,* I added silently. *Please tell me why. Tell me you lost my number or were in a car accident or got abducted by aliens. Anything . . .*

"Yeah, I know. . . ." Josh's voice trailed off. As quickly as he'd grabbed my hand just a moment ago, he now let it drop to my side.

"Josh?" Why wasn't he jumping up and down or

introducing me to his friends or gluing his lips to mine? "Josh, what's going on?"

He was looking over my head, his blue eyes intent. "Raleigh," he said.

I spun around. Raleigh was standing right behind me. And she was beaming at Josh. "Hi, babe!" she chirped happily. "Great game."

"Thanks." Josh stepped away from me as if I'd just announced that I'd recently been exposed to the Ebola virus.

I watched in horror as Raleigh threw herself into Josh's outstretched arms. "Hi, Sara," Raleigh greeted me after she finally unclenched her hands from around Josh's biceps. "Did you meet my boyfriend?"

Boyfriend? Oh, God. "I, uh, I . . ." This wasn't happening. This wasn't my life. Some mistake had been made, and the universe had handed me some other girl's romantic crisis.

"We met," Josh said. He gave me a quick glance, then put his arm around Raleigh's waist.

This was going from bad to very bad to the absolute worst. The corn dog felt like lead in my stomach.

Suddenly Tim was at my side. "Sara, are you ready to go home?" he asked, his chocolate brown eyes filled with concern.

I nodded silently, unable to speak.

"Let's go, then," Tim said. I vaguely heard him exchange good-byes with Josh and Raleigh while I felt as if I were going to faint. I probably would have collapsed if Tim weren't there to hold me up.

But thank God he was, because I needed to escape as soon as possible. I needed to get away from the crowded stadium, away from Josh, and away from the pile of garbage that my life had suddenly turned into.

"How—could—he—do—this?" I gasped in between large sobs.

The car ride home had been a complete blur to me. I'd been such an emotional wreck for the past hour that I barely knew how I'd made it to the end of the short wooden dock that Tim and I were now sitting on. Nor did I care. The only thing I did know was that I'd never been so angry, hurt, depressed, or heartbroken in my life.

I usually never let myself cry in front of other people. Or cry at all, for that matter. But after what I'd just been through, I couldn't help it. I was a blubbering fool. And the way Tim sat there, patiently listening to me, made me feel that it was all right to cry as much as I wanted to. Who would've thought there was such a caring guy behind that teasing demeanor?

Tim sighed and shook his head. "Because he's a jerk, Sara. That's how."

But he *wasn't* a jerk. He was Josh, the guy I'd fallen in love with. Even though I'd witnessed it with my own eyes, it was still impossible for me to believe that the Josh who'd been holding Raleigh's waist was the same Josh I'd been with all summer.

I stared out at the Atlantic and wrapped my arms around my knees. As I attempted to wipe my eyes dry I was struck by a sudden hopeful thought: My Josh would never do something like this. There had to be some sort of explanation. What if—

"Maybe they just started going out," I began, glancing over at Tim. "I mean, maybe Raleigh broke up with that longtime boyfriend of hers and she and Josh are a recent rebound thing. Josh must've been devastated when he couldn't get in touch with me and—"

"Raleigh and Josh have been together forever," Tim interrupted. "They're, like, *the* Glendale couple."

"Oh," I whispered. My eyes blurred with tears once more as I plunged headlong back into depression. This couldn't be my life—this couldn't really be happening to me. I pinched myself just to make sure. Oh, yeah, this was a nightmare come true, all right.

"I thought Josh loved me," I said, almost to myself. "I know I loved him. . . . He was the first guy I ever felt that way about."

"What a jerk," Tim muttered.

"He's more than a jerk; he's a—a— How could he do this to me!" I cried once again, slamming my fists down on the dock.

"Some guys are just extremely stupid," Tim said. "And Josh is the leader of those guys. Listen, Sara, the best thing you can do is forget all about Josh Nelson. Just forget he even exists."

I looked at Tim and dropped my legs down into

the water. It seemed to have a calming effect on me. I let out a shaky sigh. "You know what? You're right. I'm going to make Josh a memory."

"Good."

But as I glanced up at the bright Florida moon, my stomach twisted in nauseating turns at the mere thought of eliminating Josh from my life. How could I possibly do that? "What if I never get over him?"

"You will. Believe me."

"I don't think so, Tim. Jerk or no jerk, I fell in love with the guy. That doesn't just disappear. I mean, look at my father—he's never gotten over my mother."

Tim let out a small laugh. "That's a little different. Your father and mother are both great people who just weren't right for each other. It's been hard for your dad to let go of that. But he will eventually once he meets the right person. Josh, on the other hand, is just some loser who doesn't deserve you to so much as glance in his direction."

I was quiet for a moment, taken aback by how insightful Tim was about my parents. He probably knew more about them than any of my friends back home since he spent so much time with my father. Then I realized that Tim had actually gotten me to forget about Josh for a millisecond. Maybe I *could* possibly get over him.

"All right," I said quietly. "The jerk is history."

Tim squeezed my hand. "That's the attitude."

But even as the words came out of my mouth, I

knew they weren't true. All it took was one flash of an image of Josh gazing into my eyes, one quick memory of us kissing on our private island, and Josh was anything but history.

Sure, I could try to forget about him.

But the truth was I just wanted him back.

Haikus for Josh . . .
Which He Will Never Read

"Endless Summer"
Morning hike with you.
Tennis in the afternoon.
Nights are for kissing.

"Meeting You"
I jumped guy to guy.
Then I saw you that first day.
Nothing is the same.

"Dissed and Dismissed"
I thought you loved me.
But your eyes told careless lies.
Now I trust no one.

Five

I WASN'T LOOKING for Josh in the hallways of Glendale on Monday morning. I was *not* searching every face of every body that sped by me in the flurry before the first bell. Right. And I hadn't spent an extra thirty minutes fixing my hair this morning or tried a new shade of lipstick either. Pathetic. I was plain, old-fashioned pathetic.

Josh has a girlfriend, I told myself for the millionth time since Friday night. *He's a lousy, awful jerk who you wish you'd never met.* Right again. Those bright blue eyes had been haunting my every thought since that horrible moment at the football field.

"Get over it, Connelly," I said aloud as I forced myself to move in a more or less determined manner down the corridor. "Move on and move up."

Josh wasn't even my type. Sure, he was good-looking and smart and funny. But he was also a jock whose idea of a good time was crashing around a field while girls in short skirts shook their pom-poms on the sidelines. In fact, Josh was worse than the average jock. He'd *lied* to me.

"Hey!" My stride was suddenly cut short by a large, hard object. I whirled around, ready to be extremely rude to whoever or whatever had gotten in my way.

Instead my breath caught in my lungs. The object was none other than Josh, former love of my life. I swallowed what would have been an audible gasp in a girl with less self-control.

Get lost. Eat dirt. I knew I should spit out those words in a venomous spurt. But then his hands came around my waist.

Josh looked around to make sure no one noticed us, then pulled me backward into a janitor's closet. After all of those weeks of longing, we were alone. The crowded halls of Glendale High seemed a hundred miles away. . . . Josh always made me feel as if we were the only two people on the planet.

"Sara." What emotion did Josh's voice hold? Regret? Guilt? Although I hated to admit it to myself, I hoped it was lust.

"Hello, Josh." My heart was pounding, but I forced myself to take deep breaths. Josh had a girlfriend! The guy had to pay.

I just wished he didn't look so . . . amazing.

He reached for my hand, but I dropped his arm and glared at him. "I can't believe you're here," he said.

"In the flesh." *Literally.* I was glad that I was wearing one of my skimpier tank tops. The thin black straps showed off my well-shaped arms, and the low neckline highlighted what little cleavage I was proud to call my own.

"You're beautiful—just like always." Josh took a step closer.

I inched backward but didn't get very far. A stack of mops and brooms kept me from moving deeper into the closet. Josh was so close that I could hear him breathing.

Stay strong, girl. He's a con artist. "And you have a girlfriend."

"We have to talk." Even in the dim light of the small storage closet Josh's blond hair appeared soft and shiny. My fingers ached to touch it.

I wasn't going to get into any cheesy conversation about good times, fond memories, and ships passing in the night. Josh had treated me like a fool, and I wasn't about to forget it. "I didn't know you played football," I said, changing the subject.

"You told me the first day we met that you thought football was a brutal sport. You said—and I quote—'it appealed only to guys who had a deep need to prove that their heads were hard enough and empty enough to suffer major brain damage.'" He was staring at me. I mean, really *staring*. My heart skipped a couple dozen beats as I tried not to get lost in the deep pools of his eyes.

"So you remember." That meant something. I wasn't just some cheap summer fling—Josh could quote me. Unfortunately the guy was also all too familiar with lying. He'd lied about Raleigh, he'd lied about not being a football player. For all I knew, he was really a girl in man's clothing. I couldn't trust a word that came from his mouth.

"I remember a lot of things, Sara." He took another step in my direction. There wasn't much more distance to cover.

I scooted away, dodging several buckets and a dustpan. But now my back was pressed up against the door—I could feel the cold metal doorknob digging into the small of my back. "Really?" I was falling, falling, falling.

He seemed to sense my weakness. "We can't talk here," he said. "And we can't talk now."

Where was a witty response when I really, really needed one? My mind was blank. "Okay." *Good one, Sara. Way to go.*

"Meet me tonight," Josh said. "I'll be at the Mandarin Boulder at eight o'clock."

I had no idea where the Mandarin Boulder was, but I knew that nothing would keep me from there tonight. "I'll be there," I promised. "I mean, I'll see what I can do," I amended in a chillier voice.

All right, so it had taken a few seconds, but my cool had kicked back in. The old Sara was lurking somewhere inside me. I just had to find her before eight o'clock tonight, when I had a feeling that those piercing blue eyes would be looking at me with a gaze so heated, it would put Fabio to shame.

Now . . . what was I going to wear?

★   ★   ★

By 7:53 P.M. the small map that Tim had drawn

for me was a crumpled mess. Of course, I'd committed the route to the Mandarin Boulder to memory within five minutes of receiving the directions. I still felt a little guilty about telling Tim that I was going to the spot to take pictures for my intermediate-photography class. But I knew he'd just try to stop me from meeting Josh.

As soon as I pulled my Oldsmobile into the small gravel parking lot, I realized why Josh had chosen this spot for our rendezvous. The Mandarin Boulder was huge and lay at the edge of the ocean, surrounded by over a dozen smaller rocks. This was the landscape of the coast of Maine.

I felt a rush of homesickness as I slammed the driver's-side door shut. In Maine the September night air would be chilly. Here the temperature was still a balmy eighty degrees. And I couldn't help but notice that palm trees, rather than pines, lined the side of the road that led to this small cove.

I didn't see Josh. Maybe he was going to blow me off. Maybe this was his way of telling me once and for all that I'd been a fool to think that he cared about me one iota this summer. Maybe—

"It's a long way from Lake Vermilion, huh?" Josh had appeared—seemingly out of thin air.

He was standing a few feet in front of the boulder, wearing nothing but a pair of faded khaki cutoffs and a small navy blue backpack. Oh, man, nothing beat the sight of a beautiful guy in a good pair of shorts.

I race-walked to get to Josh's side as quickly as

possible. "So. I'm here." Now I was out of breath and realizing that I appeared way overanxious. Big surprise.

"I'll help you up." Josh held out one hand and tilted his head up to the giant boulder. Six weeks ago I would've grabbed his hand, pulled him close, and probably given him a hug just for the fun of it. Today I settled for only part A. I clasped the long fingers of his hand and heaved myself onto the rock.

Neither of us said a word as we climbed to the top of the Mandarin Boulder. At least, no words were spoken out loud. I was having an unpleasant one-way conversation with the back of Josh's head as I struggled to keep my feet in my new Day-Glo thongs. *You're gorgeous. You're a worthless human being. You're everything to me. No, you're nothing to me.* The mental babbling went on and on.

When I reached the top of the boulder, I saw that the semiarduous climb had been worth the effort. The Atlantic Ocean stretched out before us, glittering in the fading sun. I might have been hallucinating, but I was almost positive that I saw dolphins jumping in the distance. Oh, he was striking a low blow. Who could be angry amidst all this nature?

"I'm sorry I didn't tell you about Raleigh," Josh said. "I meant to explain the whole situation to you, but somehow I never found the right words."

I leaned back on my elbows and stared out at the sea. "You lied to me."

"I didn't *lie*, exactly. I just neglected to tell you the whole truth." He pulled a bottle of Poland

Spring water from his backpack.

"That's a crock," I responded. "You let me believe that you felt the same way about me that I felt about you. I mean, I even told you that I . . ." My voice trailed off as the words caught in my throat.

"I know, I know." Josh didn't want me to say the words either. How could I have been so stupid last summer? I should've known not to tell a guy I loved him before he told me. That was, like, war-of-the-sexes rule number one.

"Are you in love with her?" I hadn't meant to ask. I had, in fact, sworn to myself that I wouldn't. Josh didn't deserve a question as emotionally loaded as that one. Why did I care whether or not he loved the cheerleader of the year?

He was quiet for what felt like an hour but was probably more like ten seconds. "I don't know," he said finally. "I thought I was—and then I met you."

"Oh." Wow. This wasn't the response I had expected. Or maybe it was. Maybe that was exactly why I had allowed myself to ask the question. But I definitely hadn't anticipated the sincerity that I heard in Josh's voice.

"Raleigh and I grew up together," Josh went on. "She was the first girl I ever kissed . . . the first girl I even *thought* about kissing."

"That's way more information than I need," I interrupted.

Josh sighed. "Sara, I wish I could tell you that Raleigh and I are going to break up. I wish I could ask you out on a proper date and put my arm around you and introduce you to my parents."

"But?" I hated my voice. I sounded like Marge Simpson on helium.

"But none of those things are possible. Raleigh and I . . . well, everyone expects us to be together. I can't let them down." Josh took a long drink from his water bottle and offered it to me.

The gesture was simple, but it brought tears to my eyes. Raleigh Stockton was the girl who had access to all of those casual, endearing gestures—a ride to school, an apple at lunch, a squeeze of the shoulder. I had nothing but an album of poor-quality snapshots.

"What does 'be together' mean, exactly?" I asked. "They can't expect you to go out with the girl for the rest of your life."

Josh was silent for several long moments. "You have to understand—Raleigh and I have all the same friends. I mean, we're practically an institution at Glendale." He shrugged. "And I'd be lying if I didn't say that our parents are hoping we'll get married someday."

Married? We were only seventeen, and already the guy was planning his wedding. The only thing that was worse than Josh's idiotic prediction of marrying Raleigh was the fact that I'd spent the last several weeks fantasizing about my own marriage to Josh.

"You let me give you my address," I said softly. "Knowing that you'd never write me one lousy letter, you let me give you my address." I giggled, one of those hysterical she-needs-to-be-on-Prozac giggles. "I even gave you my phone number. . . . I actually thought you were going to *call* me."

"I would've written to you eventually." Josh's warm, tanned arm slid around my shoulders, which only made me feel worse. In fact, I was close to tears.

You will not cry in front of him; you will not! I ordered myself. I turned my face away from Josh. "Whatever," I whispered angrily.

This was so unfair! Josh had already broken my heart once. Why did I have to be dragged here just so he could rub Raleigh in my face a little more? Didn't he know how much it hurt me to think about him so much as holding hands with someone else? I wanted him to know exactly how that felt. I wanted him to—

I whipped my head around and glared at him. "You know, you're not the only one who's been cheating, Josh," I blurted out without thinking.

Oh, no. Oh, God. Did I really just say that?

Josh went pale. "What do you mean?"

Oh, yeah, I did.

"I . . . uh . . . have someone else too." Now that I'd started, there was no way I could stop. And when I saw how upset Josh looked, I didn't want to. "He means everything to me."

"Really." He didn't disguise the hurt and anger in his voice. Hurt and anger, two emotions I was now all too familiar with. Take that, Josh.

"Yes." Jeez, I was almost convincing myself.

His eyes were intense as he stared at me. "I can't think about you with someone else. It's . . . awful."

I wanted to regret the lie. But how could I? Josh's jealousy meant everything to me. "I guess we're even, then. I feel the same way about Raleigh."

"Who is he?" Josh asked, his voice raising several decibels. "Tell me who he is."

Yeah, Connelly, I thought, *who is he?* "That's not important."

"Look at me, Saraphina." My heart melted. *Saraphina.* Josh had used that nickname for me all summer.

I turned my head a fraction of an inch. "We have nothing to talk about," I whispered. "Don't worry, I won't give your secret away. Raleigh will never find out what you were up to all summer."

He shook his head. "That's not what I'm worried about." Josh's lips were almost unbearably close to mine now. "I'm afraid that I won't be able to keep myself from doing this. . . ." His mouth touched mine, sending a high-wattage bolt straight down my spine.

"No, we can't," I whispered back. *Don't go there, Connelly. Don't do this.*

"It's totally wrong for me to kiss you . . . right?" Josh hadn't moved away from me. If anything, he had edged closer. Our legs were almost touching.

"Right." I ignored the throbbing of my pulse in my throat, almost scared to speak. There was no doubt that the tremble in my voice would give away just how badly I wanted to feel his lips against mine.

"I've missed you." Josh's voice was a hoarse whisper against my ear. His hands roamed everywhere, taking my breath away.

"Josh . . . Josh." I knew I should tell him to stop kissing me, but my brain had floated somewhere far away from my head.

"Sara, you're so beautiful. God, I missed having you near me." His fingers were tangled in my hair, and I slipped my arms around his waist.

I pulled him closer, aching to feel every one of his muscles against me.

He drew his mouth away. Had we been kissing for only a moment or for an eternity? I had no idea. "I shouldn't have done that."

"No." But oh, it had felt so good. I tried to picture Raleigh's kind, friendly face. All I could conjure up was the image of an annoyingly cute button nose and hair-sprayed bangs.

"I have to go." He jerked his body away from mine and rose to his feet. "Good-bye." And in an instant Josh had disappeared over the side of the boulder, leaving me to find my own way down.

My heart was still pounding, and I felt as if I needed several tanks of oxygen pumped into my lungs. I was both devastated and exhilarated—a dangerous combination in any girl. But I would manage to find my own way down. And I would continue to find my own way, no matter what happened between Josh and me.

Sara Ponders the Meaning of Dreams . . . and Nightmares

Last night I dreamed that I was swimming in the ocean, except that the water was warm—almost like a bath. I was wearing a wet suit, and my body was weighted down with scuba-diving equipment. The only problem was that I couldn't actually scuba dive because I didn't know how. Meanwhile Tim was somewhere deep below the surface of the water, having the time of his life as he studied various fish and plant life.

As I was treading water, waiting for Tim, I saw Josh surf by on a surfboard that was so small, it looked more like a ski than an actual board. He called out to me, but I couldn't hear what he was saying because the waves were crashing so loudly. Once he was gone, the image of Josh was replaced with a giant shark's fin. I screamed and forgot that I was supposed to be moving my legs in the murky water. I started to sink.

The shark came closer and closer. I was sure I was going to drown, but at the last second I felt Tim's arms circle my waist. Then I woke up.

Various shrinks and gurus say that all dreams are meaningful. One woman told me that if you put yourself in the place of every object in your dream and view the dream from that object's point of view, you can interpret whatever it is your subconscious is trying to tell you. I tried to do that with this nightmare, but I just came up with a jumbled mass of confusion.

I have an irrational fear of sharks. Let's just say I never should have rented Jaws *with Maggie in seventh grade and let it go at that. Okay?*

Six

"SARA, ARE YOU listening?" Tim asked, probably not for the first time, Tuesday afternoon. He was in the middle of giving me a run-through of scuba-diving terms in order to prepare me for my first lesson in the water.

I blinked and glanced around my dad's cozy living room. "Uh, yeah. You were saying something about air defibrillators."

He shook his head. "A defibrillator is the thing Noah Wyle uses to bring a guy back to life after he's been run over by a car. I was talking about an air decompresser."

"Right, right." So I was a little spacey. It happens to the best of us. Or, in my case, the worst of us.

I'd spent the last twenty-four hours in a complete fog. Last night I'd driven home from the beach in a state of total mental pandemonium. For the first couple of minutes of the drive I sat stiff behind the wheel, cringing with horror that I'd lied to Josh about having a boyfriend. *What if he finds out the truth?* I'd wondered. Then I'd look like even more of a desperate idiot. But for the next couple of miles I reminded myself of how jealous Josh had looked when I'd told him. And I began to smile so wide at the memory of Josh's kiss that I kept seeing flashes of my big white teeth in the rearview mirror. Then I dissolved into tears. As amazing as the kiss had been, it had also been our last. Josh had hurt me more than any guy I'd ever known.

Now, a few feet away, Tim tossed aside a pair of flippers and flopped onto the worn green sofa. "You've got to stop thinking about that jerk already. It's a waste of your time. And to tell you the truth, it's a waste of mine. You haven't heard a word I said."

"Yes, I have. And I was *not* thinking about him. I was simply making a mental note to tell my dad that he should have that crack in the wall checked out."

"Uh-huh." Tim stretched out his legs, folded his hands behind his head, and closed his eyes. Within seconds he was snoring.

Huh. My scuba-diving instructor had just fallen asleep midlesson. This was certainly an unexpected turn of events. Apparently I'd become so boring that not even Tim could deal with my company while in a conscious state. Maybe Josh found me just as boring.

I walked over to the sofa and nudged his shoulder. "Tim?" I called softly. "Tim, are you awake?"

Out of nowhere his hand shot from his side and he grabbed my wrist. "Miss me?" The strength of his fingers surprised me. "Miss me?" he asked again.

I jerked my wrist from his grip. "What are you trying to prove?"

He sat up. "I'm making a point," he said. "You're so out of it that you might as well be asleep, and unless I've missed something, *I'm* the one who's doing *you* the favor." He raised an eyebrow. "I could be watching the baseball game with Ed and Soren right now."

Where was the patient Tim of the other night? This Tim definitely believed in tough love. Still, I knew his intentions were good—he just wanted me to get over Josh.

"Sorry, sorry. The jerk is forgotten." *Yeah, right.* I picked up one of the scuba-diving masks Tim had brought over and stuck it on my head. "I'm ready to pay attention now, Your Majesty."

Tim gave me a quick, skeptical once-over. "I think you mean you're ready to *pretend* that you're actually listening to anything I have to say."

I pulled off the mask and tossed it onto Tim's lap. "Last night I kept having shark attack nightmares." This was true, but I was also using the dream confession as a means of steering the conversation away from my MTV-like attention span due to Josh.

81

Tim groaned. "This lesson is a farce. Let's forget it for tonight."

I shrugged. "Fine. How about we cook some real hamburgers on the grill, then?" My dad was spending the evening at an artists' colony thirty miles away, leaving open a rare opportunity for me to eat meat without being lectured about chemicals and cruel breeding conditions.

"I'll make you the best hamburger you've ever tasted," Tim offered. "On one condition."

"What's that?" I asked, my mind suddenly drifting. Josh and I had cooked burgers together. Burgers and hot dogs and chicken. I could almost smell the A.1 sauce as I thought about those cool Maine nights. . . .

"You have to clue in to our dinner experience and quit thinking about that guy—like you are right at this moment."

I blinked back at Tim. "I was *not* thinking about Josh."

"Right. And I'm not thinking about the fact that I'm alone with a beautiful girl for the first time in over a year."

Okay, awkward pause. Major awkward pause. "Uh . . . what?"

Tim grinned. "Just wanted to make sure you were listening."

"You're a jerk, you know that?"

He just kept grinning. "Well, you *are* beautiful, if misguided."

"Thanks for nothing, Kaplan." But I had to laugh—he definitely knew how to get me.

Tim stood up and headed toward the kitchen. "So, do you want to fire up the grill or what?"

"Sure. And for your information, it won't be long until I'm totally and completely over Josh," I told him, desperately trying to convince myself that the kiss Josh and I had shared had been a bittersweet good-bye kiss of the Romeo and Juliet variety. Josh was unavailable, and I was moving on. Period.

Tim stopped in the doorway of the kitchen and turned around. "You do know that Josh isn't worth all the mental energy you're expending on him, don't you?"

What was he talking about? Except for the small fact that he'd lied to me, Josh was practically perfect. "You're wrong about that. Josh is an amazing guy."

"Josh is charming. He's popular. He's a great athlete. But he's nowhere near amazing." Tim stared at me for a moment. "Just take a look at how he treated you."

"You don't even know him!"

Tim shrugged. "I've had a few classes with him. We were actually bio lab partners sophomore year. I know him well enough." With that Tim walked into the kitchen.

I stood in the middle of the living room, feeling deflated. Tim was wrong. He had to be. There was no way I would have chosen to fall in love for the first—and possibly only—time with a guy who fell under the bar of amazing. I was too smart for that. Wasn't I?

Oh, man. Life had never been this complicated in Maine. I was a mess, and I had no one to turn to. At least no one in this town, in this house, in this room. Tim was clearly sick of hearing about Josh. But I did still have a best friend. Right after dinner I would call Maggie and ask for advice. And comfort.

Wednesday afternoon I pushed my way through the as-per-usual packed hallway of Glendale High. I couldn't stop thinking about Clarissa Dalloway, the protagonist of the book my AP English class was reading. In *Mrs. Dalloway,* Virginia Woolf had created a character who was as different from me as anyone I could possibly imagine. I mean, poor Clarissa was a stuffy English lady who spent most of her time fretting over flower arrangements and silver polish.

But I related to the way Clarissa felt as if the balance of her whole life were hanging by an invisible thread. At one point Virginia Woolf described Clarissa as "oddly conscious of her hat" as the character exchanged some simple interaction with a man on the street. That was exactly how I felt— oddly conscious of *everything*. Did anyone know that I was secretly in love with Josh? Did other kids look at me and see the anguish in my eyes as I made my way listlessly through the halls? Tim had picked up on all of this. . . .

I stopped in front of my locker and forced myself to take a few deep, cleansing breaths. *I am not self-conscious. I am not self-conscious.*

The note stuck into my locker caught my eye immediately. And I had no doubt who it was from. I picked up the small white square and unfolded it with the care one might show to a first-edition copy of *The Iliad*.

I almost didn't want to read the words Josh had written. If this was good-bye . . . then it was good-bye. Right now, poised before his scrawling hand-writing, the possibilities were endless.

Dear Sara,
I have to see you—I can't stop thinking about you. I know things are complicated, and that's my fault. But you can't shut me out. You just can't. Meet me at the fortune-teller's booth at the board-walk on Saturday at noon. Please.

Josh hadn't signed the note. He didn't need to. I read and then reread the letter a dozen times, my heart pounding so fast, I thought I might have a heart attack.

Then I remembered Tim's words: *The best thing you can do is forget that Josh even exists.* I crumpled up the piece of loose-leaf paper, determined to throw the note away and expel its contents from my mind forever.

Inhale. Exhale. Who was I kidding? This note was going nowhere but straight under my pillow. I quickly decrumpled the precious piece of paper and smoothed it out as much as possible. Then I care-fully folded it into a small square, kissed it, and stuck it into the front-left pocket of my Levi's.

Josh and I hadn't lost the magic that flowed between us at Camp Quisiana! The emotions were still there, as strong or maybe even stronger than they'd been over the summer. I pushed the image of Raleigh's friendly smile out of my head and breathed a sigh of relief.

Josh and I were going to be together after all. A girlfriend had been an obstacle in our path, to be sure. But obstacles were romantic and tortured and provided wonderful dramatic plot points. Now Josh was ready to break up with Raleigh, and I was ready to take on the world.

Hot sun warmed the top of my head as I circled Madame Zona's fortune-teller's booth on Saturday. This was my first trip to the Bay Beach boardwalk, and so far I was disappointed by the sparse array of rides and games. There was a small, decrepit roller coaster, some run-down bumper cars, and a row of games. Still, this was the place where I would see Josh, and I knew that I would therefore hold the image of this boardwalk close to my heart for the next forty or fifty years.

If only Josh would show up. I glanced at my watch, already knowing that the big hand had moved past the six. Josh was a full half hour late.

Three months ago I wouldn't have waited five minutes for a guy. I would have arrived at the fortune-teller's booth, noted that Josh hadn't shown up on time, and taken off to meet Maggie at the mall. End of date, end of story, end of guy. Now I was lingering at the boardwalk like a puppy stranded by the side of the highway. Pathetic.

Uh-oh. Sleazy dude at three o'clock. I looked off in the distance, praying for a lightning bolt to strike him down. No luck. The guy was staring at me with an oily smile. I could already hear the lame pickup lines.

He was drawing closer and closer. "Hey, sweetie, how about we go for a ride in the Tunnel of Love?"

I stared at the guy's neon pink Surf Naked baseball cap. "Get lost," I told him.

"Hey, babe, I'm just makin' friendly conversation." Mr. Surf Naked leered at me from behind the longest, greasiest bangs I'd ever seen.

"You heard her. Get lost." And it was as seamless as that. One moment Josh had been the bad guy who had stood me up for what was arguably the most important date of our entire screwed-up relationship, and the next moment he was my hero. Ah, sweet love.

Josh took a step toward Mr. Surf Naked, highlighting the fact that he was at least two inches taller and twenty pounds more muscular than my unfortunate suitor. The guy backed away, defeated. "Sorry . . . I, uh, didn't know she was taken."

Josh glared. "Well, she is."

A warm tingle traveled up my spine. I was taken. I loved feeling "taken," even if it was by a guy who already had a girlfriend. Once again standard nineties feminism became second to nineteenth-century romanticism. Oh, well. I turned to Josh. "Thank you."

He grinned. "No problem."

I gazed into Josh's eyes, trying to remind myself that he was half an hour late and I was furious with him. But all I could think about was how gorgeous he looked in Levi's cutoffs and a white button-down oxford-cloth shirt. "So where were you?" I forced an accusatory edge into my melting voice.

His eyes dropped to the ground. "I'm so sorry. I, uh, got held up at home."

Josh's alibi had Raleigh written all over it. "How stupid do you think I am? I know you were with Raleigh."

"Let's sit down if we're going to talk about this." Josh grabbed my hand—no, I didn't protest—and led me to a small wrought-iron bench at the edge of the boardwalk.

"You're the one who wanted to see me today," I said as I sat down. "You're the one who left that note in my locker, not the other way around."

"I did want to see you. . . . I *do* want to see you," Josh started, running his hands over his hair. "But I didn't know when I left that note that my parents had invited Raleigh and her family over for brunch this morning. There was no way I could get out of it."

The image of Josh, Raleigh, and their collective parents sitting down to pancakes and bacon made me want to throw up the Raisin Bran I'd eaten that morning. A sudden rage came over me. I hated Raleigh. I hated her parents. I hated Josh. I hated Josh's parents. I hated *everyone*.

I was not going to let Josh get my hopes up again only to remind me that his girlfriend took up all his time. The guy had to suffer.

"Listen, I had to break a date to get here today," I heard myself say. "But I was on time."

Oh, man. Why did I do that?

Once I saw the flash of jealousy in Josh's eyes, I knew *exactly* why I'd lied. "What date? With who?" he demanded.

"With him," I said. "With the guy I told you about the other day." Okay, I'd really entered the realm of the absurd now, but who could blame me?

"I thought that guy was in Maine!" Josh practically shouted. "He lives in *Florida?*"

I nodded, both horrified and pleased by Josh's reaction. "Yes, he does. We met a couple of years ago . . . at Disney World." I'd never even been to Disney World, but there seemed no reason to stay grounded anywhere near reality at this point. "Anyway, we, uh, wrote letters and talked on the phone all the time. When I found out I was moving in with my dad, we knew our romance was destined to be."

"Tell me his name," Josh demanded.

My mind was a blank. *Name, name, name. Any name will do.* "His name is Tim," I blurted out without thinking. "Tim Kaplan." *Uh-oh. Big uh-oh.*

"Tim Kaplan is your mystery man?" Josh exclaimed. "You're going out with Tim Kaplan? My bio-lab partner?"

Oops. "Uh, yeah."

"So *that's* why you were with him at the football game," he said.

"Uh-huh." I gulped. "That's why."

"This is bad," Josh whispered. "This is very, very bad."

You have no idea just how bad, I silently answered Josh.

I glanced at the fortune-teller's booth. I knew exactly what Madame Zona would have seen in my future. Disaster. Somehow I was going to have to convince Tim to pretend to be my boyfriend. And I had a sinking feeling that this was going to be a task that even Xena, Warrior Princess, would find challenging, if not impossible.

Seven

AFTER ANOTHER HALF an hour of discussion Josh and I had decided that we might as well go on with our date. After all, we were already out and at the beach. And neither of us had other plans or anything. . . .

Okay, any normal two people would have stopped their date at the point when each had proclaimed their love for another person. Any normal girl would have recognized that by lying through her teeth she had embroiled herself in a very awkward situation and bowed out with as much grace as she could muster. Apparently neither Josh nor I was normal. So I had called my dad and told him not to expect me home until late. Yes, I admit it—I was weak. The truth was that I wanted to be with Josh, and logic wasn't going to stand in my way.

Josh and I spent the next few hours playing arcade games, stuffing our faces with cotton candy, and riding the somewhat dilapidated roller coaster at the boardwalk. It was the kind of afternoon that I'd dreamed about when Josh and I had been separated by most of the East Coast.

"Today was awesome," Josh said to me now. "I felt like we were back in Maine, before any of this other stuff happened."

"I know," I answered, sighing. "It's amazing."

We were sitting on the beach, feasting on a dinner of Pringles, smoked-turkey sandwiches, and Dr Pepper. Food had never tasted so good. The sun had set over an hour ago, and the sky was thick with stars as usual. Aside from a few not-so-minor details, life was perfect.

"Let's talk," Josh said, pulling me close to his side.

I settled into his warm embrace and rested my head lightly against his shoulder. "What do you want to talk about?" I murmured. All weighty topics seemed to have slipped into the sea and washed away with the tide.

"Us." His arm tightened around me, and his lips brushed lightly against my forehead.

I sat up straight. "What about us?"

"I think we're in love." Josh said the words so casually that at first I wondered if I'd misheard some irrelevant comment he was making about the nice weather. "At least, I know I'm in love with you."

My heart was a drumbeat. This was the real deal. "I love you too," I whispered.

"But we're both committed to other people,"

Josh continued. "I can't break up with Raleigh . . . not yet anyway. And you said that you don't want to hurt Tim."

Okay, so my lies hadn't stopped at the wrought-iron bench. Maybe I *had* gone on and on while we were standing in line for the roller coaster about how much Tim loved me. And perhaps I'd mentioned that Tim had said if I broke up with him, his life would become meaningless and he'd be compelled to quit school and move to Golden Gate Park in San Francisco, where he'd set up a tent and live off nothing but dandelion seeds and tree bark. I've always had a pretty active imagination—it's not an easy thing to turn off once I've been given an opportunity to elaborate.

"Uh-huh . . ." I was still reeling from Josh's declaration of love. Actual speech beyond a few cavewomanlike grunts seemed impossible.

"But we want to see each other. We want to spend time together." He turned his head and looked into my eyes the way only Josh could do. "We want to be able to kiss each other the way we did under the pier."

There went my heart again. That kiss under the pier had lasted a full twenty minutes. "Uh-huh . . . ," I repeated stupidly.

"So I was thinking that maybe we *can* continue our relationship. We could go out with each other in sort of an . . . untraditional way."

"Untraditional?" I asked. "What does that mean?"

93

"We could see each other secretly," Josh answered. "Like we did today."

I should have gotten up and walked away. No, I should have slapped Josh across his face, *then* gotten up and walked away. But I didn't. I just sat there like an idiot. "Oh."

"I mean, eventually we'll go out like a regular couple," Josh continued hastily. "But this will give us time to let down Raleigh and Tim softly."

"I don't know," I said. I couldn't get myself to muster up an actual no.

Josh shifted in the sand so that we were face-to-face. "Say yes, Sara. Please."

He was begging. Josh was actually *begging* me to cheat on my boyfriend so that we could be together. The fact that I didn't have a boyfriend was irrelevant. He had a girlfriend—a nice one. An inner debate raged within my mind. To say yes to Josh's proposal would go against everything I believed in. But to say no would deprive myself of the thing I wanted most in the world.

"I do love you," I whispered. "But I can't hurt Tim." Had I just said those words? Jeez, I was beginning to convince *myself* that Tim and I were a hot-and-heavy item. Why on earth had I ever gotten myself into this mess?

I stared into Josh's blue eyes. Oh, yeah, that's why.

"No one ever has to know," Josh said.

That wasn't quite true. I had to tell Tim something. And I seriously doubted that he was going to agree to go along with my lie at all, much less without forcing me to tell him the exact reason for it. Tim was way too smart to believe that I wanted him to act like my boyfriend just for the fun of it. He always saw right through me—the guy had X-ray vision into my soul.

"Sara, we have to be together." Josh put his hands on either side of my head, then drew my face toward his.

The pact was signed, sealed, delivered, and notarized by the time our lips touched. I would agree to see Josh in secret. I knew it. He knew it. And somewhere in the universe I was sure that whoever controlled the forces of karma knew it too. But I couldn't say no. And I would find a way to make Tim understand that this was important to me. I had to.

What am I going to tell Tim? What am I going to tell Tim?

The same question repeated itself in my head again and again as I sat on the end of my dad's dock. Now that I was away from Josh, the utter absurdity of my lie had been able to sink in. How could I have let this go so far? And how would I ever get Tim to go along with it?

"Are you mooning over Josh—or just enjoying the moon?"

Startled, I looked up to find Tim walking toward me. "Tim! Hi!" Was my voice unnaturally bright? Was it obvious that I was trying to hide my guilt for involving him in my lie?

"I guess scuba-diving lessons are about one hundred and one on your list of priorities," Tim said softly.

Oh, man. I had completely forgotten that I'd promised Tim I would go to the beach for another lesson today. As soon as I'd received Josh's note, any other plans for the day had simply vanished from my mind. It was now nine o'clock, and scuba diving was totally out of the question.

"Tim, I'm so sorry. I, uh . . ." My voice trailed off. We both knew that there was no way I was going to extricate myself from my screwup in any dignified manner.

"That was some kiss," Tim said, filling in the moment of silence. "I'd give it a ten, except that Josh isn't a deserving contender."

"What?" My eyebrows shot up. "When did you see us kiss?"

"I went to the boardwalk after you blew me off," Tim explained. He sat down next to me on the dock. "I wanted to check out the work of a local artist who sells his stuff down there."

"Oh." Boy, did I feel stupid.

"What are you doing with Josh, Sara?" Tim reached down and slipped off his flip-flops, then plunged his feet into the cold ocean water. "I thought we agreed that he was history."

"I know, but, well, I'm . . . I'm in love with him. We're in love." Okay, that much was true.

"He broke up with Raleigh?" Tim asked. "I can't believe it."

I wished more than anything that I could respond yes to that question. "Not exactly," I responded instead. "He doesn't want to hurt her."

Tim glanced at me. "In that case, why is he kissing you?"

"We, uh, have an understanding." This had all seemed so logical when Josh and I were sitting on the beach. But now I was feeling slightly nauseous. And giving Tim all the gory details was going to make me feel even worse.

"What *kind* of understanding, dare I ask?"

"We're going to see each other . . . discreetly . . . until Josh has a chance to let Raleigh down easy."

"Are you insane?" Tim asked, his voice high. "That's—that's . . . totally and completely scummy."

All right, now he was making me mad. Sure, this wasn't the shining moment in my life as a worthwhile human being. But everything I was doing was for the sake of love. "You've obviously never been in love. If you had, you'd understand what it's like—what it can make you do."

He shook his head, staring at me with disbelief in his eyes. "Are you listening to yourself? You sound like a character on a bad soap opera."

Wow. He was not going to let me off easy. I started to panic. What if he didn't agree to go along with my lie? "Please don't tell anyone you saw me kissing him, Tim."

He sighed deeply. "I should, but I won't." He paused. "Satisfied?"

I nodded. "Uh, there is one other thing. . . ." I

winced, bracing myself for what I was about to ask of the best friend I'd made since moving to Florida.

I knew what I was about to request of Tim was completely horrible. But I had to do it—the thought of Josh finding out that I'd lied was just too painful to contemplate.

"I'm afraid to ask," Tim said dryly.

I took a deep breath. *Here goes.* "I told Josh that you're my boyfriend," I said quickly, hoping that sheer speed would take away from the impact of the words.

"You *what?*" Tim exclaimed. "Why?"

"I don't know. I just did." How could I explain the jealousy that had been eating away at my guts since the night I saw Josh put his arm around Raleigh at the football game? There was no way to make Tim understand the most base of human instincts that had made me desperate to hurt Josh the way he had hurt me. Even I didn't understand.

"Well, you're going to have to *un*tell him," Tim said. "I don't want any part of this sordid triangle."

"I can't." My voice was barely a whisper, but it was firm. "It's too late."

"Why?"

"Because I told him all sorts of stuff—how we met at Disney World, how you wrote me almost every day for the last two years. . . ."

"You're really insane, you know that?" I thought I detected a hint of amusement in Tim's voice. "You're an original, Sara."

98

I was almost positive that I had seen Tim's mouth curve into a soft grin. "Are you smiling?" I asked.

He shrugged. "What can I say? Insanity is funny."

"Does this mean you'll go along with the idea that we're a couple?"

He stared at me for a long moment, his brown eyes burning coals. "That depends. Do I get the benefits a boyfriend would get?"

Benefits? Did he mean what I thought he meant? *Of course he does, Connelly; what else would that mean?* For some stupid reason, my heart began to pound at the thought. "Uh . . . no. I mean, we're not *really* going out, so I don't think that—"

The intensity slipped from Tim's eyes. "Relax, Sara. I was just kidding."

"Oh, okay. I mean, yeah, I knew that." So why was my heart still pounding? I looked away from Tim's gaze and forced myself to concentrate on the issue at hand. "So, you'll do it?"

Tim nodded. "For you, I'll do it." He paused. "But don't think I approve. I thought you were better than this. I guess I was wrong."

I felt an unexpected pang of sadness at Tim's reproach. But I pushed it to a deserted corner of my mind and focused on the fact that I'd gotten what I wanted. Warmth and relief flooded through me. It was going to take a little time, but with Tim's help everything was going to work out just as it had been destined to.

Dear Maggie,

It's after midnight, and I have a calculus quiz tomorrow. But how can I sleep? At last things are starting to come together. Josh and I have proclaimed our everlasting love and have promised to stay together forever. Okay, maybe I'm embellishing a little, but you get the drift.

Re our convo on the phone the other night: Of course Matt is telling the truth when he says he likes you more than any girl he's ever dated. And I'm sure your new haircut isn't as bad as you think. But just say the word and I will FedEx you my wig. I know how important a good head of fake hair can be in these situations.

Did I mention lately that Tim is a saint? I can't believe I ever found that guy annoying. He's totally helping me out with Josh (I'll explain later—it's too complicated to go into in a letter). I watched Tim work on my dad's pottery wheel the other day. He made a vase that he said he's going to give to his mother as a congratulations gift for her new promotion at work. Pretty nice, huh? If you weren't totally into Matt, I might even suggest a little fling between you and Tim when you come to visit (when, by the way, are you coming to visit?).

Tell everyone I say hi and send my love. I never realized how much I appreciated all our friends until I came to a place where I don't know anyone. Thank goodness for Tim. If it weren't for him—and Josh, of course—I would spend many a Friday night watching Star Search *reruns and eating microwave popcorn. As it is, life is going from bearable to good to great all within the space of a few weeks. Isn't life crazy?*

Love,
Me

Eight

WEDNESDAY AFTERNOON I walked toward the Glendale High parking lot, humming the tune to my dad's favorite Bob Dylan song, "Baby, I'm in the Mood for You." I was in the mood, all right. I was in the mood to spend hours and hours with Josh.

Love was, indeed, a many-splendored thing. Since the Saturday night Josh and I had spent at the beach, I'd been walking around in such a blissed-out state that my dad had asked if I was lacing my morning coffee with Saint-John's-wort. Even my mom had noticed my euphoric state of mind when I'd talked to her on the phone. But why shouldn't I be euphoric? Last week we had managed two actual dates—one movie and one late dinner. We had even ditched lunch one afternoon and made out at the beach.

Last Sunday, Josh and I had whispered to each

other on the phone for almost two hours. Last night we'd met at "our" rock for forty-five kiss-filled minutes. Plus Tim had kept his mouth shut as promised. He'd even walked down the hall with me a couple of times when I knew Josh would be around.

And pretty soon Josh would break up with Raleigh and we wouldn't have to sneak around anymore. Then I could shout the words to any number of sentimental love songs for all of Glendale High to hear. I couldn't wait.

"Hey, Anna!" I called to a curly-headed girl who sat next to me in calculus. Finally I was starting to feel like an actual member of the community at school. Slowly I was making friends.

"Will you be at the game on Friday?" Anna called back.

"Wouldn't miss it." She didn't know how true that was. Although I still wasn't crazy about the idea of guys running around a field in order to beat up on one another, I loved watching Josh race toward the end zone in his white football uniform.

I waved to a few more people as I entered the still crowded parking lot. Of course, it was going to be easier to make real friends once Josh and I became official. As it was, I always felt as if I were hiding something from other kids.

"Oh, yeah, baby, I'm in the mood for you," I sang, heading for my car. My voice broke off as my stomach turned suddenly into a tight, twisted knot.

The love of my life was fifty feet away, and he wasn't alone. Josh and Raleigh were standing next to her white Cabriolet convertible. They were clutching each other like a couple of extras treading water on the set of *Titanic*. A familiar sensation, one of wanting to throw up my most recent meal, washed over me.

Josh's hands were tangled in Raleigh's dark brown hair, and her arms circled his waist, pulling him close. They did *not* look like a couple on the verge of the breakup of the century. Witnessing this tender moment, an objective outside observer would no doubt come to the conclusion that Josh and Raleigh were very much in love. Hot tears of both anger and sadness sprang to my eyes.

I sprinted the rest of the way to my car and yanked open the door. Out of breath, with tears rolling down my cheeks, I lay on the black vinyl seat, wishing with all my might that my eyes had deceived me. I slid up a few inches on the seat and peered in the rearview mirror. Josh and Raleigh were still in a lip meld. Ugh. Gag. Puke. Vomit. Yuck.

I dropped back down. This was an all-time low for me. Here I was, lying in my convertible, hyperventilating and sobbing. Maggie would never believe that I had sunk to these depths. This simply was *not* me.

Closing my eyes against the glare of the afternoon sun, I allowed reality to come crashing down. Things between Josh and me *weren't* wonderful.

Our so-called relationship was an utter joke. Tim had been right all along. I never should have agreed to be the other girl in Josh's life, even if the situation was only temporary.

I had to find a way to make Josh realize that he had to choose me and me only.

"Have I told you lately that you are totally out of your mind?" Maggie asked on the other end of the phone four hours later. "I mean, you've done some crazy stuff in the past, but I think the Florida sun is melting your brain."

I reached down to scratch Georgie on the ears as I thought about how to respond to Maggie's statement. Sure, my plan was pushing the edge of what most people would consider decent behavior, but in this case the end justified the means. "Mags, you don't understand what it's like to have the guy you love so close—yet so far away."

I'd retreated to my room immediately upon returning from the dreadful parking-lot incident. For two hours I'd delved into the darkest corners of my mind, searching for a plausible way to make Josh drop Raleigh to go out with me. When inspiration finally struck, I'd called Maggie for advice and support. So far she was offering neither.

"Sara, this plan is like the plot of some straight-to-video movie. First you tell Josh that you have a boyfriend, which you don't. Then you go out with Josh secretly, continuing to pretend that you're also going out with this nonexistent guy—"

"Tim isn't nonexistent," I interrupted. "He's real." Georgie wagged her tail at the mention of Tim's name. My dog had formed a love for Tim that was so obvious, I was almost jealous.

"The fact that he's *real* makes matters even worse," Maggie continued. "Now you want to make poor Tim put on some ridiculous show so that you can drive Josh to the brink of insanity—"

"At which point he'll realize that he can't live without me, dump Raleigh, and become my boyfriend," I interrupted again. If I didn't keep Maggie's monologues moving, she could talk for hours. On the other end of the line I heard Maggie sigh.

"Can I ask you something?"

"Sure." Maggie was a little flaky at times, but she always made pertinent comments. And from the sound of her tone I had a feeling that I wasn't going to like whatever question she was about to ask.

"Where does all of this leave Tim?"

"Tim? What do you mean? Tim will be *relieved* that the whole thing is finally over."

"Hmmm . . ." Maggie didn't sound convinced.

"Trust me," I said. "Once Josh and I are a couple, Tim will dance for joy that he doesn't have to keep up the whole boyfriend act—not that he's done much acting yet."

"I'm not so sure about that," Maggie said slowly. "And pardon me for pointing out the obvious, but Tim sounds like a guy with a heck of a lot more integrity than Josh. He may not be so willing to be an active participant in your melodrama."

"But there's no other way," I insisted. I'd gone over and over the whole mess in my mind and come to the conclusion that only through a tiny bit more deceit would I be able to live a life that was free and clear of guilt, existential torture, and heartbreak. I had to make Josh so jealous by doing the girlfriend-boyfriend thing with Tim that he couldn't stand the idea of me going out with another guy. Then he would break up with Raleigh, and this whole farce would become a memory.

But first things first. In order to make Josh crazy jealous, I intended to tell him that things were over between us and then give him some major cold shoulder. In my experience guys didn't respond too well to getting blown off by a girl who was supposedly their number-one fan.

Another long, dramatic sigh. "You're determined to go through with this, aren't you?"

"Yep. It's the only way to show Josh that I'm not some dim-witted girl who's content to hang out on the sidelines while he plays house with Miss Miami Dolphins Cheerleading Squad wanna-be." Georgie laid her head in my lap and gazed at me with sympathy in her chocolate brown eyes.

"So, what's the next step?" Maggie asked.

"Somehow I have to get Tim to agree to lay on the boyfriend stuff extra thick," I answered. "I mean, he has to seem like he's totally head over heels in love with me."

"That *will* make Josh jealous," Maggie conceded. "If it's done correctly."

"But how do I get Tim to agree to it? He's already fed up with me and my lies."

"Simple," Maggie said. "You throw yourself at his feet and beg for mercy."

Now I was the one who sighed. Sometime in the very near future, I was going to have to ask Tim for yet another favor. And if he said no, I was going to lose Josh forever.

Thursday afternoon I pulled at the tight fabric of the wet suit Tim had loaned me for our lesson. He'd decided that I knew enough about the art of underwater exploration to get near the ocean, although he still wasn't ready to let me go on an actual dive. Which was fine with me. Even though I'd gotten a rush from trying out the breathing apparatus standing waist deep in the Atlantic, I still wasn't too psyched about the prospect of wandering around at the bottom of the sea.

"You know, you might have a future as a scuba diver after all." Tim tossed the tank of air he was holding onto the sand and plopped down beside it.

"Really?" I grinned. Getting anything that even approached a compliment from Tim was no easy feat. "You think so?"

He smiled. "Yeah. Just as long as you quit having those dreams about sharks in the shower. Fear underwater can be deadly."

"A few measly dreams aren't going to keep me

from conquering the sea, Mr. Serious Instructor. And it's not fair to use privileged information against me."

Tim pulled down the top of his wet suit, revealing the wiry muscles of his arms and torso. "True enough. I won't say another word."

"Speaking of not saying a word . . ." I'd been searching for an entrance point to ask my latest favor of Tim, and this seemed like as good an on-ramp as any.

His eyes immediately clouded. "Great." Long pause. "What is it now?"

"This thing with Josh isn't right," I said slowly, sitting down beside him on the soft white sand of the beach.

Tim looked up to the sky. "Hallelujah! At long last the girl sees the error of her ways!"

I cleared my throat nervously. "Which is why I need to, um, facilitate the process of him breaking up with his girlfriend."

"Facilitate the process?" Tim asked. "That sounds bad—whatever it's supposed to mean."

"Josh is jealous of us," I explained. "But up until now he hasn't really had to deal with the fact that you and I are a couple. I mean, sure, he knows it, but he doesn't *know* it."

"First of all, you and I aren't really a couple. Second, I don't like the way you're looking at me. I feel like a mouse on the way into a boa constrictor's mouth."

"Just hear me out," I begged. "Please."

"Do I have a choice?" Tim yanked off his fins and dug his toes into the sand.

"I need us to act more like a couple so that Josh will be blind with jealousy," I explained. "You know, flirting, holding hands, blah, blah, blah."

Tim raised one eyebrow. "The blah, blah, blah part sounds interesting. Do we get to make out in the hallways of Glendale?"

I ignored the blush that I was sure was spreading over my face. "I'm not falling for that, Kaplan. I can tell when you're teasing."

Now was not the time to mention that an actual kiss might at some point become a necessary element of the role playing I was requesting of Tim. I'd spring the lip-to-lip action on him later. Tim's eyes lost their mischievous gleam. "Seriously, haven't I done enough to help you out? I mean, I don't even *like* Josh. I don't want you to go out with him—he doesn't deserve you."

I'd heard Tim say all of this before, but not with the intensity that was now in his voice. Panic swept over me. Was it possible that Tim would refuse to cooperate with me? No. He simply *had* to agree. Suddenly my wet suit felt as if it were strangling me. The stakes had never been so high, and I was starting to hyperventilate.

"I have to be Josh's girlfriend," I said in between pants. "It's the most important thing in the world to me."

"*Why?* Why is this such a big deal?" Tim asked. "I mean, you spent a lousy couple of months with

Josh. Raleigh has known him for ten years."

I forced myself to take a deep breath to slow my breathing. In. Out. In. Out. "I told you before that I love him."

Tim shook his head. "I'm not buying that. There's more to this." He paused, gazing out at the ocean. "Your obsession with Josh has gone beyond whatever you think you two shared during your summer fling. You're more focused on winning than on anything else."

I blinked back at him, surprised. How was it that he had this uncanny ability to pick out my most vulnerable spot and hone right in? We hadn't even known each other that long. But what he said was true—even Maggie had pointed it out during our phone conversation the night before. The intensity of my passion had spiraled out of control. Still, I couldn't let go of my dream. Not yet, and maybe not ever.

"I don't like to lose, Tim," I said quietly. "I believe that if I want something badly enough, I can achieve it. And I want Josh."

He turned to look at me. "You're crazy, Sara, you know that?" His brown eyes had softened now. I could tell that his resolve was shifting as he ran his fingers back and forth in the sand.

"I know," I said, unable to keep a smile from spreading across my face. "Now, are you with me?"

"Yeah," Tim agreed. "But if this whole charade doesn't end soon, and I mean *soon,* then it's over. Period."

"Deal." I put out my hand for Tim to shake. When his fingers clasped mine, I pulled him closer and put my arms around his shoulders.

Tim hugged me close, then pulled away so that we were staring at each other, eye to eye. "Will you do me one favor?"

"Anything." How could I refuse my savior?

"Don't lose yourself in all of this. Don't forget that at base you're a good, kind, open-hearted person."

"How can you think I'm any of those things after everything you've seen me do?" I asked softly.

Tim gazed at me. "It's my artist's eyes. I look beyond the surface and see into the soul."

My pulse raced as I looked away from Tim and stared down at the fabric of my wet suit. I hoped my soul survived this next round of deceit and manipulation. I was definitely pushing the limit of what a person could do and still maintain good karma.

Just a few more days, and then I'll turn back into the honest Sara. This was do-or-die time. I was going to succeed, or I was going to crash and burn. Either way the nightmare would soon be over.

Nine

I THOUGHT MY heart would burst out of my chest as I stood in front of the Nelsons' front door on Friday afternoon. I knew that Josh was home—all the football players were ordered by Coach Wilson to rest for at least an hour before a game. In just seconds, I would implement phase one of my new and improved plan to get the man of my dreams. I just hoped I had the guts to go through with it.

The doorbell rang unnaturally loudly. It was one of those that played a tune—this one was "When the Saints Go Marching In." The whole neighborhood was probably aware of my arrival. Unfortunately it wasn't Josh who appeared at the door.

A tall, blond woman stood in the doorway, gazing at me quizzically from head to toe. "Can I help you?" she asked.

For a moment I couldn't speak. This was the first time I'd been face-to-face with either of Josh's parents, and this was hardly the kind of introduction I'd hoped for. *Hi! I'm the girl your son has been kissing behind his girlfriend's back for the last couple of weeks. May I come in?* Yeah, right.

"Uh . . . is Josh home?" *Great. Way to make a poised first impression, Connelly.*

She frowned. Did I have "other woman" tattooed across my forehead? "He's resting right now, dear."

But then Josh appeared behind his mother. "It's okay, Mom. I'll just talk for a minute."

Mrs. Nelson shrugged but retreated without saying anything more. I breathed a sigh of relief. The first obstacle had been conquered. Now on to the second, bigger hurdle.

"Hi, Josh."

"What are you doing here?" He didn't look too happy to see me. There was no mind-numbing kiss or warm embrace or even a half smile.

I flipped my long blond hair over one shoulder and reminded myself that I looked absolutely fabulous in the light blue sundress I'd chosen for this monumental occasion. "Hello to you too."

"I'm sorry . . . it's just . . . do you think it's a good idea for you to be here? Raleigh is coming over before I have to leave for the game—"

"This won't take long," I interrupted. If he thought I was going to slink down the front walk like some kind of kicked puppy, he was nuts. There was no law that said I couldn't stand on Josh's porch.

"Okay, um, I'd ask you to come inside, but my parents—"

I waved my hand. "I don't need to grace your living-room sofa with my presence to tell you what I have to say."

"What's wrong?" Josh asked. His voice had softened, and he was sounding more like the guy I'd fallen in love with at Camp Quisiana.

"I'm finished with this charade," I said icily, borrowing Tim's word. "I want a *real* relationship. I want to meet your parents and go to school dances with you and go to a movie with you on Friday night."

Stop thinking about his amazing blue eyes, I ordered myself. *Remember, this is all part of the grand plan.*

"Sara, we've been over this. . . ."

I averted my gaze from the delicate golden hairs on his tanned forearms and continued. "And I don't want to kiss another girl's boyfriend while I'm parked on the side of some deserted road where no one will see us."

I was really getting warmed up now. All the frustration of the last few weeks bubbled to the surface. The experience was turning from nerve-racking to empowering to eerily real. I almost, and I stress *almost,* felt as if I were telling Josh that things were over between us for real.

"You know I can't break up with Raleigh yet, and you can't break up with Tim." He stepped outside and shut the door behind him. Unfortunately this small movement meant our bodies were just inches apart. My newfound anger started to slip away.

"Josh, I'm serious. It's her or me. Your choice."

My voice was unnaturally high as I swallowed the bucket of tears that threatened to spill from my eyes.

"You can't ask me to choose. It's not fair." His bright blue eyes were begging me to let this go.

"All's fair in love and war," I said. "I can't go on like this."

His hand reached for mine, but I took a step backward. Any form of physical contact was going to render this whole thing null and void.

"I'm leaving now," I said through the tears. "I'll see you at school on Monday. Maybe."

"You can't just come here and dump this on me," Josh insisted. "Let's get together tomorrow and talk this thing through."

I'd been prepared for this. And I knew that any private rendezvous with Josh would result in me aborting my carefully thought-out plan. I shook my head. "There's nothing to talk about until you and Raleigh are officially broken up."

I pivoted on the heels of my platform sandals and walked quickly toward my Oldsmobile. It was imperative that I get as far away from Josh's house as possible. My heart felt as if it had just been reamed by a sledgehammer.

"Sara, I love you," Josh called softly.

I was so close to turning back around and rushing into his arms that my sandal-clad feet actually started toward the door. But then my brain caught up to my body, and I continued back down the brick path. I wasn't going to give up. I couldn't.

Josh was still standing in front of his house as I

revved the engine of my convertible and peeled off from the curb. I had said everything I'd promised myself that I would. As of this moment Josh and I were through. At least, that's what I wanted him to believe. And starting Monday, we would be on a rough road toward reconciliation. I was counting on it.

On Monday at noon the weather gods were on my side. The usually sunny Florida days often pushed Glendale students out onto the school grounds at lunchtime. But today there was rain, and every senior was packed into the cafeteria. I had exactly the audience I was looking for. Tim and I were standing side by side in the lunch line, and I was whispering instructions to him as we made our way through the selection of entrées, sides, and desserts.

"I don't think I can do this," Tim said, choosing a haggard-looking piece of German chocolate cake from the uninspired dessert display. "I'm no good at acting."

"Just follow my lead," I hissed. "There's nothing to it."

I grabbed a small bowl of vanilla pudding and wished that I felt half as confident as I sounded. In truth, I'd never had to actually seek out attention before. Usually all eyes naturally found their way to me and whatever I was up to. Now I was about to stage a performance—one that needed to look so real that Tim's and my supposed romance would be on the tongues of everyone in this cafeteria.

We moved toward the cash register in silence,

and I nudged Tim with my elbow. "Ready?"

He handed the cashier a five-dollar bill. "Nope."

I thrust four singles at the lady, not bothering to wait for my change. "Good. Let's go." I stuck my tray into Tim's hand—boy carrying girl's tray was almost a sign of engagement at Glendale.

"Sara . . ." His voice was pleading, but I was already positioning myself so that Josh, who was sitting at a nearby table with half of the football team, would hear every word I said.

"Tim, don't say that!" I shrieked, squeezing his arm. Then I let loose with a giggle worthy of Cameron Diaz in *My Best Friend's Wedding*. "You know I'm not the kind of girl who does *that!*"

Tim's face was red, but he managed an impish grin. "Will you at least come over to watch a movie with me when my parents go out of town this weekend?" he asked. "I promise I'll be good."

I sighed and ran a hand through his dark hair. "Maybe. But only if we can watch *When Harry Met Sally*." It's a well-known fact that any movie with Meg Ryan is a girl's flick. If a guy is willing to submit himself to that kind of sap, it's a sure sign that he's head over heels in love.

"For you, Ms. Connelly, I'll even rent *Sleepless in Seattle*." Tim was gazing at me with such convincing adoration that I was close to forgetting he'd been dragged into this plan with the proverbial kicks and screams.

I snuck a quick glance at Josh's table. My victim was watching us, all right. And his blue eyes were so filled with anger that I half expected him to leap from his chair and shove both of the trays of food Tim was carrying into my so-called boyfriend's face. Instead Josh shot me a look that made my heart do a somersault. I love intensity, drama, and passion, and this moment was filled with all three.

Tim and I continued toward an empty table at the far end of the cafeteria, whispering and giggling. When we finally slid into our chairs, I noted with an extreme amount of satisfaction that Josh's gaze hadn't wavered. His eyes had followed Tim and me across the room.

"Great job!" I told Tim. Then I leaned over the table and pretended to whisper in his ear, keeping up the act. "You're a natural."

Following my lead, he took my hand in his and smiled. "I can hide my true emotions as well as the next guy—when I need to."

I nodded. Tim was one pleasant surprise after another. If the Academy gave out an award for flirting, he would have been this year's Oscar winner. Despite the fact that I had no appetite, I picked up my grilled-cheese sandwich and took a huge bite. The sandwich wasn't bad . . . but victory tasted even sweeter.

One hour and sixteen minutes later I stood outside the door of my AP English class. We were about to finish our study of *Mrs. Dalloway,* and I still felt "oddly conscious" of just about everything about myself. But this afternoon I was basking in the glow of my hyper-self-awareness.

Several girls had already approached me to say that Tim and I were one of the cutest couples in school, and I'd noticed more than one guy glancing enviously in Tim's direction as we exited the cafeteria. Tim's friend Soren had even yelled something along the lines of, "Way to go, dude!" So far, so great.

Up the hall I saw Josh turn the corner. I just happened to know that he had U.S. history four doors down from my English class this period. I smiled at him as he approached. "What was that all about?" he demanded.

I batted my eyelashes and leaned against the lockers behind me. Wisely I was wearing a short skirt with the kind of strappy sandals that made guys lose all power of speech. "Excuse me?" I kept my voice cool but cordial.

"You and Tim Kaplan—you were practically making out in the middle of the lunchroom. . . . It was disgusting." Josh's face was the color of a ripe tomato, and I noticed a few veins popping out from the side of his neck.

I shrugged and glanced at my watch, as if there were a thousand places I would rather be. "I was exchanging friendly banter with my boyfriend. It's commonly known as flirting, and it's a normal human activity."

Josh collapsed against the lockers and let his history textbook fall to the floor. "Cut it out. I'm serious."

"So am I." I glanced at my watch again. "Is

there something you wanted to say?"

"I want to say plenty of things," Josh sputtered. "I thought you loved me, and now you're carrying on with that artist guy like he's Leonardo DiCaprio or something."

"As you know, Tim and I are a couple." I tapped my foot against the tiled floor and assumed the kind of bored look I imagined Clarissa Dalloway had when she spoke to the servants at her London town house.

"I don't want you going over to his house this weekend!" Josh practically shouted. And he wasn't looking around to see if Raleigh was nearby. This was a first—usually he didn't speak to me without making sure that we were completely alone. "He's going to take advantage of you—I can feel it."

I rolled my eyes. "One: I'm a big girl, and I can take care of myself. Two: Tim is a wonderful guy who would never do anything of the sort you're suggesting." I glanced one more time at my watch, just to make sure he got my initial point about having better things to do with my time. "Three: None of this is any of your business whatsoever."

Josh's mouth opened and closed, but no words came out. Man, he was sexy when he was angry, jealous, and speechless. I wanted to fling my copy of *Mrs. Dalloway* to the floor and jump into his arms. Instead I gave him my best Mona Lisa smile. "Now, if you'll excuse me, I have to get to class."

I turned and sauntered toward the door of the classroom, aware that Josh's eyes were burning a hole through the back of my tight red T-shirt. *Take that, Josh.* I swayed my hips a little and flipped my hair over one shoulder. *And that.*

"This isn't over, Sara," Josh said to my retreating back. "This thing between us is nowhere near over."

At the door of the classroom I turned. "I guess that's up to you, isn't it?"

"Sara . . ." He practically moaned my name—a tingle traveled from the top of my head down to the tips of my toes.

"You better go find your girlfriend," I said coolly. "If you're out of her sight for more than ten minutes, she might report you missing in action." With that I slipped into the classroom and bounced toward my regular seat.

On a scale of one to ten, this day had been a nine. And as soon as Josh came to his senses and dropped Raleigh, I had a feeling that I was going to experience more tens than Michelle Kwan at an amateur skating competition. *Yes!*

Hey, S.,

Yes, it's true. I'll be in Florida exactly one week from today. Can you believe *it*? Thank goodness for teachers' conferences—three-day weekends rule!

Anyway, my mom said that I was spending so much on long distance that she might as well buy me a plane ticket. I think that she misses you herself and wants a report on how you're doing down there.

Matt is taking me out for dinner the night before I leave—he already asked me. I'm so psyched. . . . I think he's going to kiss me. Yeah, I know I've been kissed plenty of times by plenty of cute guys. But Matt's different. I don't know—let's just say I haven't even thought about the possibilities for guy watching on the Florida beach. Does that mean I'm in love? Is this how you feel about Josh—all warm and tingly and peaceful?

Love,
Mags

Ten

"I STILL DON'T understand what we're doing here," I said to Tim on Tuesday afternoon as I followed him across a wide expanse of beach that lay a mile from Glendale High.

"If you can hang on for all of about thirty seconds, our mission will become clear," he responded.

"If you say so." I slipped off my shoes, which had already filled with sand, and continued across the beach.

Tim was in a mood I'd never seen him in before—he was almost giddy with excitement over something. After school he'd met me at my car and insisted that I drive him to this spot by the ocean. I'd tried to question him about this journey, but Tim had just pointed to the rather bulky backpack he was carrying and told me to shut up and drive.

Tim stopped suddenly and dropped his backpack

onto the sand. "Look that way," he told me, pointing north.

I glanced up the beach. About a hundred yards away, twenty guys were racing back and forth across the sand. "What's going on?"

Tim grinned. "I happened to overhear Chuck O'Sullivan say that the coach was bringing the football team down to the beach for a full afternoon of wind sprints."

"Aha." This was nothing short of a miracle. Tim had taken it upon himself to further Operation Push Josh Over the Edge. I never would have thought he had the capacity for such proactive devious behavior lurking within. I was impressed. "So are we going to sit here and wait to be noticed?" I asked.

Tim shook his head. "Nope." He knelt in the sand and unzipped the backpack. "There's something I've been wanting to try for a long time, and today is the day that I'm going to try it."

I was definitely intrigued. Tim wasn't the type of guy to shroud himself in mystery—at least, I hadn't thought so up until now. Clearly there was a lot about Tim I didn't know. "I'm dying of curiosity, Kaplan. Don't keep me in suspense."

I'd already picked Josh out from among the other football players. He was wearing a pair of loose black shorts and a faded yellow T-shirt. My hope was that after running a dozen or so sprints, he would be compelled to strip off the shirt. Despite our current chilly status my mouth watered at the thought of an unobstructed view of Josh's rippling muscles.

Tim pulled out a huge chunk of clay with a flourish. "I'm not just your dad's assistant, you know. I also like to think of myself as something of an artist."

"You're a great artist, and you know it," I told him, sinking onto the sand while keeping one eye carefully glued to the football team.

I'd been stunned the first time my father showed me a collection of the things Tim had created on the potter's wheel. Having grown up studying my dad's work, I knew quite a bit about pottery. And there was no doubt that Tim's vases and pots showed a talent that far exceeded his age and experience.

"Usually I work on the wheel," Tim said, placing the clay onto a large white cloth. "But this afternoon I'm going to do a sculpture."

"Of what?" I asked, still gazing at the football team. I wished I could take a bottle of water over to Josh. He looked exhausted.

"You."

My head swiveled from the vision of sprinting football players to Tim, who was kneading the clay with his long, slim fingers. "Uh, me?"

"Yep." Tim glanced up and smiled at me. "You're going to be my muse."

I was shocked. "I don't know. . . . I've never thought of myself as the model type." Sure, I had a healthy dose of self-esteem, and I was used to being admired by leering guys. But no one had ever *studied* me. No one had ever created a work of art based on my likeness. The idea was quite intimidating.

Tim began to shape the clay. "Just think about how jealous Josh will be when he notices us over here and sees that I'm staring at your face as I mold your delicate bone structure with the tips of my fingers."

"Hmmm . . ." I hadn't thought about Tim's project in that light. He had an excellent point. "I see what you mean."

"Great. Let's get started." Tim studied my face for a long moment. "Look toward the ocean and tilt your chin up a little."

I followed Tim's orders, although I was disappointed that my pose forced me to take my eyes off Josh. "Is Josh watching us?" I asked.

"Not yet. But he will be." Tim fell silent.

I wanted to keep talking, but it was obvious that Tim was intent on his work. I stared out at the water, reflecting on my new friend's amazing change in attitude. His performance at lunch yesterday had been superb. And now this. For a guy who had claimed he didn't think Josh was worthy of my affection, Tim was certainly going all out in order to help me win back my summer love. Why?

As the minutes passed, I became less and less aware of Josh and the rest of the football team. I heard faint echoes of their grunts and moans as they ran their sprints, but I was mostly listening to Tim's quiet sighs as he labored over the sculpture. Posing for Tim felt surprisingly natural—almost like meditating.

"He's looking," Tim said suddenly. "And Nelson looks seriously upset."

"Really?" I was dying to break my pose, but I forced myself to stay frozen in place.

"Yeah." Tim was quiet for several seconds. "Now the coach is yelling at him."

"Great!" I felt a rush of gratitude toward Tim. If he hadn't come up with this brilliant afternoon plan, I would have wasted the entire day without taking a step toward my ultimate goal.

What was Josh thinking right now? Did he feel as much pain seeing me with Tim as I had when I happened on him and Raleigh kissing? To any passerby, Tim and I probably looked like any normal couple. No one could know that our romance was total fabrication. Even *I* sometimes forgot.

"Josh just stormed out of practice," Tim reported. "And he shot me a look that you would *not* believe."

There was no way I was going to rob myself of this sight. I abandoned all pretense of being absorbed in my modeling and turned to see Josh. He was jogging away from the football team toward the beach parking lot. Although I could hear the coach yelling after Josh, I couldn't decipher exactly what he was saying—which was probably for the best. Guilty feelings were building at a rapid rate. Still, this was what I had wanted . . . right?

Josh turned around to glance at Tim and me one more time, which prompted me to jerk my head back to the other direction. If Josh knew I took every opportunity to stare at him, he might become just the least bit suspicious of my so-called romance. "Mission accomplished," I commented.

Tim's hands smoothed the clay under his fingers. "Happy?" Tim was molding what would become my nose.

I nodded absently. "Very." Shockingly enough, I was even more mesmerized by Tim's sculpture than I had been by the spectacle of Josh's untimely exit.

"Now that Josh is gone, are you going to insist we leave?" Tim asked. "And move your head back toward the ocean as you ponder that question."

I did as he said, then shook my head slightly. "I would never interrupt a genius at work," I told him, barely moving my lips as I spoke.

Tim laughed softly. "You're an all right girl, Sara, you know that?"

"Nah . . . I just want to see my face displayed at the Metropolitan Museum of Art someday, that's all."

Tim didn't respond. In fact, I didn't think he had even heard me. He was already absorbed in his work. I sighed softly. My dad was like this when he worked—his tendency to lose himself in art for days at a time was one of the reasons my mother had finally left him.

Of course, Tim had already shown me that he didn't totally block out the world when he was occupied with a piece of art. He had taken the time to notice Josh watching us. And Tim hadn't made one sarcastic comment when I craned my neck so that I could see Josh leaving practice. I owed the guy big time.

In the near silence that followed, I could sense Tim's gaze intent on my face. I moved my chin a fraction of an inch so that I could see his eyes. His gaze was so intense—no one had ever looked this way at me before. I felt totally exposed. And beautiful.

"Tim, why are you doing this?" I asked finally. "Why are you helping me?" When he didn't answer, I cleared my throat loudly. "Tim? Did you hear me?"

His hands stopped moving over the small sculpture. "Two reasons. One, I realize that the sooner your plan works, the sooner I'm out of this debacle." He paused for a moment, and I saw out of the corner of my eye that he was beginning to shape the lips—my lips.

"What's the second reason?" For some insane reason, my heart started to beat a little faster as I waited for his answer.

Tim shrugged. "You have the face of an angel, Sara . . . an artist's dream."

Ridiculously my heart began to pound at hearing Tim compliment me that way. His voice didn't hold its usual note of mocking irony. The blush that crept to my cheeks was coming from somewhere deep inside. Was there something more between Tim and me than just friendship?

"Sara?" Tim whispered.

I swallowed. "Uh, yeah?"

For a long moment he looked at me. "Um, just tilt your head a little to the left."

"Right. Sure." I breathed deeply and tilted my head.

Calm down, I told myself, *you and Tim are just friends.* I had simply become carried away with the game. Yeah, I was positive that was all there was to it.

Wednesday night I paced back and forth across the hardwood floor of my bedroom as I talked to Maggie on the phone. "I don't understand why you're not being more enthusiastic about all of this!" I said. "I mean, Tim and I totally pulled this thing off. I never knew the little twerp—okay, so he's not a twerp, he's good-looking—but anyway, I never knew Tim could be so deliciously *devious*—"

"Sara, are you listening to yourself?" Maggie interrupted.

I stopped my monologue but continued to pace. I was so revved up that I was having a hard time realizing that this was—theoretically at least—a two-way conversation. "What?"

"You're going on and on about what a great guy Tim is, but you haven't said one nice thing about Josh."

I stopped walking and plopped into my rocking chair. "So? Tim *is* a great guy, and I have plenty of nice stuff to say about Josh." I stuck out my tongue at Georgie, who was looking at me quizzically. Funny, I'd never noticed before how alike Tim's and Georgie's eyes were. How . . . endearing.

"Tell me something good about Josh," Maggie demanded. "And I don't want to hear another speech about his silky blond hair or his well-formed biceps." Was this the Maggie I'd been best friends with for my entire life? I'd never known her not to be interested in cute-guy details.

"Josh is funny. Josh is smart. Josh is loyal—"

Maggie snorted. "*Loyal?* I don't call cheating on your girlfriend loyal."

I wasn't sure whether Maggie thought Josh was cheating on me or on Raleigh—and I didn't want to know. "He's also a great football player." There was certainly no arguing that point. And athletic ability said a lot about a guy—discipline, grace, lung power.

"It sounds to me like Tim is the guy you should be gaga over," Maggie said, thankfully not calling me on my past tirades against football. "From everything I've heard, your artist is ten times the guy Josh is."

She was so wrong. Josh was my soul mate. "You wouldn't understand, Mags," I sputtered. "You've never been lucky enough to have the Josh experience."

There was another snort from a thousand miles away. "I hope I never do."

"Can we get back to what I was talking about, please?" I started pacing again. My adrenaline was pumping.

"Is this going to be more sadistic descriptions of poor Raleigh?" Maggie asked. She really knew how to take the fun out of a good story.

"I'm not being sadistic," I insisted. "I'm merely pointing out that I saw her and Josh arguing in the hall the other day—something about him being grouchy and preoccupied."

Maggie sighed. "I don't think Florida is doing great things for your karma, Sara."

I glared at Georgie, who seemed to be staring at me in an accusatory manner. "Listen, you'll see Josh for yourself when you come to town this weekend. If you still don't think he's worth all this effort, then I promise you can say as many bad things about him as you want to."

"Don't make promises you can't keep, Connelly." On the other end of the line I could hear Mrs. Gold yelling at Maggie to get off the phone and finish her English paper. Some things never change.

"I won't have to worry about keeping the promise," I assured my best friend. "I know you're going to love him as much as I do."

I was also positive that by the end of the weekend, Operation Push Josh Over the Edge was going to be over and done. I had big plans for Friday night—plans that would land me in the arms of the guy I loved.

Eleven

I WASN'T TRYING to eavesdrop on Raleigh's conversation Thursday afternoon. Really, I wasn't. And if I hadn't been so comfortably settled on the floor of the library, hidden behind a huge shelf of books, I absolutely would have gotten up and moved to another spot. As it was, I couldn't help but overhear what Raleigh was saying to her best friend, Monica Sayer.

"He's taking me to Le Bon Coin," Raleigh told her. This was the key piece of information I'd been missing. I'd already gathered that Josh and Raleigh were going out for dinner and that Josh was busting his butt to make up for the fact that he'd been an abysmal boyfriend for the entire last week. But it was only now that I had learned the unhappy couple's destination.

Monica whistled. "*Très* fancy."

Raleigh sighed. "Tonight is just what Josh and I

need. Tonight we're going to rediscover that magic that's kept us together for so many years."

Not if I can help it, I thought. As of this moment Tim and I had a dinner date at Le Bon Coin for tonight.

"I'm sure you're right," Monica said. "I mean, you and Josh are meant for each other. Once you rekindle that old flame, you'll quit worrying that he's thinking about breaking up with you."

"Let's hope so," Raleigh said. "I can't go on like this much longer. . . . Josh just isn't all there anymore."

Raleigh sounded so sad that I felt an immediate pang of regret that I was going to ruin her evening with my presence. But nothing and no one could stand in the way of the true love that Josh and I shared. Raleigh was simply an unfortunate casualty in a war of the heart. Sooner or later she would realize that her breakup with Josh was for the best. I was sure of it.

"Sara, you are a vision of loveliness," Tim said to me from across the small table we were sharing at Le Bon Coin. "Your face is so beautiful that I almost have to look away—it's like glancing at the sun."

I rolled my eyes and leaned forward in my chair. "You sound like a character in an old movie—it's a little much."

After listening in on the important part of Raleigh and Monica's conversation I'd been stuck huddling behind the stack of books for another forty-five minutes while they discussed hairstyles of the rich and famous. When they finally left, I found Tim and cornered him by the first-floor water fountain. Once I agreed to pay for the dinner (so much for the emergency money my mom had given me before leaving for Japan), Tim had been more than happy to "take" me to Le Bon Coin.

I'd spent over an hour getting dressed and had finally selected an outfit that I knew would turn heads. My little black dress (every self-respecting female over the age of fifteen has one) had never failed me.

Tim didn't look half bad either. Actually, I was sure that a girl who didn't have eyes only for Josh would say that Tim was out-and-out gorgeous. His khaki pants and crisp white shirt made him look at least two years older, and I liked his tie—navy blue with tiny white flowers. If I wasn't mistaken, Tim had even smoothed his hair with a dab of gel.

Josh and Raleigh were already seated by the time Tim and I arrived at Le Bon Coin. I'd feigned surprise when Raleigh squealed a delighted hello at the sight of Tim and me. The stab of guilt I felt was more than dulled by my overwhelming satisfaction at Josh's obvious displeasure. His cheeks were flushed, and his eyes were bulging out of his head.

Now Tim grinned at me over the wineglass full of club soda that he was holding. "Do you want to make the guy jealous, or do you want to make the guy jealous?"

"I do, but—"

"Josh can't hear exactly what I'm saying," Tim said in a low, husky voice. "He can only hear the tenor of my words as I gaze adoringly into your eyes."

There was that blush again. I probably should have been grateful to Tim for making my cheeks turn red. From his spot at a nearby table Josh would definitely notice that I was flushed from the excitement of my supposedly romantic evening. "Okay, okay, say whatever you want. Just don't stick a rose in your teeth and ask me to tango."

Tim laughed. I saw other diners glance at our table, Josh among them. The room was lit mostly by candles, but even from twenty feet away I could see that Josh's deep blue eyes were glittering with frustration. Perfect.

"Hold my hand," I told Tim. The timing couldn't be better to up the stakes.

"What?" Tim set down his club soda with an awkward thump.

"Hold my hand," I repeated, snaking my hand across the table. "You're not afraid, are you?"

"No." Tim's fingers clasped mine loosely. "But maybe you should be."

"I, uh, what?" I was distracted by Tim's thumb, which he was moving gently back and forth across my palm.

"Even if all of this works—the plan, the jealousy, the whole thing—you might realize that Josh's touch doesn't still make your heart go pitter-pat."

I forced myself to ignore the feel of Tim's hand in mine. I wasn't reacting to this whole hand-holding thing rationally. If my emotions weren't so totally exposed at the moment, my skin wouldn't feel as if it were melting. "Trust me . . . just *thinking* about Josh makes my heart go pitter-pat."

Tim shrugged and stopped the slow circles with his thumb against my palm. "Maybe Raleigh and I can get together after your plan comes to fruition," he commented in the same romantic, lilting voice he'd been using for the last twenty minutes. "She's got a great nose. I could do wonders with it in a sculpture."

I glared at Tim. He knew I hated Raleigh's perky button nose. "You're joking, right?"

He smiled. "Raleigh is a great girl. And beautiful. Most guys would kill for a chance at a date with her, and I'll have an in. We can console each other."

Well. That had been quite an impassioned speech. As usual, I wasn't sure whether or not Tim was joking. "Excuse me, but right now *I* have a date with the ladies' room."

Tim pushed back his chair and stood up in anticipation of my departure from the table. I hadn't seen such a show of chivalry since *Titanic.* "I'll be waiting with bated breath."

I headed for the bathroom, still steaming over the comment about Raleigh's nose. Sure, she had a cute nose. But where was the verve, the personality? I couldn't believe that Tim was serious about wanting to go out with Glendale High's number-one cheerleader. She was a nice girl but totally wrong for him.

"Sara!" Josh's voice broke into my interior monologue.

I'd been so caught up in my thoughts that I hadn't even considered the possibility that Josh might follow me. I was unprepared for this obviously important moment. I stopped in the small hallway at the back of the restaurant, where the women's room was located. "Hello, Josh."

Josh came to a halt in front of me, more or less trapping me against the wall. "You and that guy are *everywhere*. Do you spend twenty-four hours a day together or what?"

His dark blue eyes were almost black, and there was a distinctly purple tinge to Josh's perfectly chiseled cheeks. "His name is Tim, and no, we don't spend twenty-four hours a day together." I gave him a small, unconcerned smile. "Is there anything else you'd like to know?"

"Why are you doing this to us?" Josh's voice was heavy with emotion. "Don't you want to be with me?"

"Maybe, but that's not the point." I gave him my most self-confident stare. "You're still going out with Raleigh, and I'm not willing to compete."

"But I explained all that." Josh clenched and unclenched his fists with obvious frustration. "God, I can't *stand* to see you falling all over that guy."

"Too bad." I started toward the door of the rest room, but Josh reached out and placed his hand gently on my shoulder.

"I love you, Sara, and I think you love me too."

"I'll see you around, Josh." I stared at him for a moment, using that sleepy gaze that had always made him grab me and kiss me during our long, hot summer in Maine. "Good-bye."

I slipped into the bathroom and leaned against the door. My thoughts were racing as I replayed the conversation in my mind. My man was about to crack. I knew that as well as I knew that the sun would rise tomorrow. I was going to get what I wanted . . . at last.

"You didn't tell me how gorgeous he is," Maggie said breathlessly. "I mean, sure, you talked about how great he is and everything, but I had no idea that he was so *cute.*"

I'd driven straight from school to the airport to pick up Maggie. I hadn't realized how much I missed my best friend until I had her right there in front of me. We had hugged each other so tightly that my sunglasses had flown off my head and landed at the feet of some middle-aged tourist guy from New Jersey. His hostile glare had cracked both of us up. Maggie and me in trouble—it was just like old times.

Now we were hanging out in my dad's back-yard, where Tim, Tim's friend Ed, and Dad were firing up the barbecue—strictly vegetarian, unfortunately. Mrs. Kaplan was in the house, putting together the salad she had brought, which meant Maggie and I had nothing to do but sit in lounge chairs and soak up the afternoon sun. I hadn't been so relaxed in weeks. For the moment I wasn't plotting or planning or scheming. I felt as if I had been reborn as my old self.

I glanced at Tim and shrugged. "He's all right if you like the type."

Maggie's red curls bounced as she shook her head. "Oh, come on. You have to admit that he's totally hot."

"I guess. . . ."

Across the yard Tim looked up from the grill. "Almost ready for that tour of my collection, Maggie?" he yelled.

"Can't wait!" she shouted back.

"Tour?" I asked. I felt a sudden, irrational pang of jealousy that they'd made plans together without me. "What tour?"

"I convinced Tim to show me his work. Apparently he has a whole garage full of pots at his parents' house."

"He's never given *me* a tour." Come to think of it, I'd never even been inside the Kaplans' house. Tim was always over at our place. Was Maggie going to go over to Tim's place when I'd never even stepped inside it? The thought of it bothered me in a way I couldn't explain.

Maggie peered at me over the black cat-eye sunglasses she'd purchased especially for her trip to Florida. "Have you ever asked for one?"

"Well . . . no." I didn't need to see every single piece of artwork Tim had created since the day he was born. I'd seen plenty of his stuff in my dad's studio.

But despite myself, I couldn't help wondering what Tim's bedroom looked like. Did he have pictures up on the wall? Was it filled with his artwork? Did he have Snoopy sheets left over from grade school on his bed? As well as I knew Tim, I'd never really glimpsed his private world. I was always too focused on me to wonder much about him.

Maggie pulled off her white T-shirt, revealing a skimpy red bikini top underneath. "Do you think it's too late in the day to get a tan?"

I raised my eyebrows. "Not if you're not worried about the indecent exposure laws we have in this state."

Maggie grinned. "I've always been a rebel." She closed her eyes against the waning sun.

"So, tell us what you think of Florida so far, Maggie," Ed called over to us from his spot by the grill next to Tim.

Maggie opened her eyes and smiled. "What's not to love? Sun, beaches, barbecues . . ."

"Don't forget all the gorgeous guys," Tim said teasingly, walking over to us. "We're a special breed down here."

Was that flirting I detected in Tim's voice? This was something new. He sounded like a total idiot. I couldn't wait for Mags to put him in his place.

"I think I need to see a little more of the Florida guys in order to comment on the male population," Maggie commented.

Tim laughed. "I think I could help you out with that."

Okay, this was getting nauseating. And disturbingly unsettling. I knew I shouldn't care, but I did not like the thought of Tim and Maggie hanging out. "Tim, don't you have a soy burger to flip or something?" I interrupted. "Maggie and I are trying to have a private conversation."

Tim took a couple of steps back to the grill. "Excuse *me*—I forgot for one second that any conversation not about Josh isn't worthwhile."

"Ha. Ha. Ha," I replied. I wasn't sure Tim had ever been quite this annoying. Apparently this was how Tim behaved when he was trying to show off for a girl.

Ed ran a hand through his thick brown hair. "I tell you, you guys have the weirdest dynamic of any couple I've ever met," he teased.

"Very funny," I responded. Ed was the only person aside from Maggie who knew that Tim and I were pretending to be going out. I just hoped my dad hadn't picked up on that comment. I wasn't up for a round of questioning. "Get back to the burgers!" I ordered both of them.

As the guys turned to the grill Maggie grinned at me. "So, tell me about Ed. He's pretty cute too."

"Ed is a nice guy, blah, blah, blah." I tried to ignore the tiny wave of irritation that was threatening to wash over me. "And Tim is not *that* cute."

All right—chill out, Connelly, I told myself. Maggie was my best friend in the whole world, and Tim was my best friend in Florida. There was no reason I shouldn't be thrilled that they hit it off so

146

well. Except for the fact that the mere idea of it made me want to puke.

"I can't wait for the party tonight," I said, ready to drop the subject of Tim for the time being. "You're finally going to get to meet Josh." Danny Sebree, the quarterback of the football team, was throwing a huge bash in celebration of the fact that his parents had gone to Europe for two weeks. "Now, tell me all about Matt."

Maggie sighed dramatically. I could practically see the thoughts of any other guy—Tim included—draining from her mind. Which, I had to admit, gave me a huge sense of relief. "He's wonderful . . . ," she began.

As Mags launched into her monologue about the virtues of Matt Brewer, I shut my eyes and settled back to listen. This was what life was all about—hanging out with friends on a sunny afternoon.

Yes, I was fairly certain that Josh and Raleigh would be at the party tonight. And if they were there, I was prepared to do something outrageous to get Josh's attention. But I wouldn't think about the major scene that might go down at the party until I absolutely had to. For now I wanted to slow down, smell the sweet salt air, and enjoy the state of just being.

Sara's Dictionary of the Five Most Important Words in the English Language

dream *('drēm), n., v.* 1. A succession of images, thoughts, or emotions passing through the mind during sleep. 2. An aspiration; goal; aim. 3. A daydream or reverie.

friendship *('fren(d)-ˌship), n.* 1. The state of being a friend; association as friends. 2. A friendly relation or intimacy. 3. A friendly feeling or disposition.

honesty *('ä-nəs-tē), n.* 1. Uprightness; integrity; trustworthiness. 2. Truthfulness, sincerity, or frankness. 3. Freedom from deceit or fraud.

love *('ləv), n., v.* loved, loving. 1. A profoundly tender, passionate affection for another person. 2. A feeling of warm personal attachment or deep affection. 3. To have love or affection for.

suffer *('sə-fər), v.* 1. To undergo or feel pain or great distress. 2. To sustain injury, disadvantage, or loss. 3. To endure or be afflicted with something temporarily or chronically.

Twelve

I'D BEEN TO plenty of parties in Portland. For that matter, I'd *had* plenty of parties in Portland. But those had been mere get-togethers compared to the bash that was taking place at Danny Sebree's. Half of Glendale High was packed into the Sebrees' living room and kitchen. The other half had spilled onto the front and back lawn.

It had taken almost fifteen minutes, but I'd finally located Josh in the crush of people dancing in the living room. He was doing a sort of modified form of slam dancing with Jeff Bernstein to Smashing Pumpkins. As usual, Josh was beyond gorgeous.

I was stationed next to the door that led from the living room to the kitchen, from where I could see both Raleigh and Josh. Typical of Glendale High's number-one cheerleader, Raleigh was manning the kitchen, where she was mixing up a batch of French onion dip. Unfortunately the girl looked great. She had discarded her goody-goody cheerleader's uniform in favor of a tight black skirt and matching tank top. I had never realized that Miss Welcome Wagon could look so, well, sexy.

I turned to Maggie, who was standing beside me. "So what do you think?" I asked.

Her gaze traveled across the room. "I think this party is awesome. Does, like, every cute guy in the country migrate to Florida?"

I laughed. "I thought you were in love with Matt."

Maggie raised her eyebrows. "That doesn't mean I can't appreciate the finer things in life—like that guy's cute butt."

I followed Maggie's line of vision. "Ah, C.J. Rouse." She was right. C.J. had a great butt. "He's going out with Eleanor Stritch."

I turned my gaze back to Josh. "So now do you understand why I'm going through all this craziness?" I asked Maggie, tilting my head in Josh's general direction.

She shrugged. "He's definitely cute."

Cute? He was way beyond cute. But how could I expect Maggie to truly appreciate Josh without having had the benefit of talking to him? She'd never heard his whispered compliments or his witty remarks. She'd never seen him run down the football field in complete command of the game.

"All right, I'm going to quit trying to convince you that Josh is my soul mate." I was tired of

Maggie's less than enthusiastic responses to anything having to do with my dream boy. "I am, however, going to show you how a girl makes the man of her fantasies the man of her reality."

"Uh-oh. Here we go." Maggie had a holier-than-thou tone to her voice, but I could see the curiosity glittering in her green eyes. She wanted to see what I was going to do as much as I wanted to do it.

"Where's Tim?" I asked. Although Tim had driven Maggie, Ed, and me to the party, I hadn't seen him since we walked into Danny's house.

I gazed around the crowded living room until my eyes found Tim. He was standing next to the stereo, engaging in what looked like a heated argument. He was probably debating the relative merits of Hole and Andy Gibb. I'd noticed that Tim's musical tastes tended toward the nostalgic.

I grabbed Maggie by the elbow and steered her toward the stereo, which took up an entire corner of the living room. I bent over a stack of discs and scanned for the perfect romantic song. When I found the ideal disc, I popped open the CD player. Good-bye, Smashing Pumpkins.

"Hey, what happened to the music?" someone yelled.

"It's coming," I called out. "Just hold on." I slipped in the disc I'd carefully selected and then walked over to Tim, slipping my arm around his waist. "Are you ready for another Oscar-worthy performance?" I asked.

He raised his eyebrows. "What did you have in mind?"

"You'll see." I clasped Tim's hand and led him toward the middle of the living room. The change in music had produced exactly the effect I had hoped for. Slam dancing had quickly turned into slow dancing.

Tim encircled my waist with his arms, and I put a hand on either side of his neck. In seconds we were staring into each other's eyes and dancing as if we were just looking for an excuse to get close to each other.

Tim pulled me closer, and I rested my head against his chest. For a few seconds I shut my eyes and gave myself up to the soft, romantic music. Part of me wished I could just dance to the song and enjoy the feel of a guy's arms around me. But I had work to do.

I opened my eyes and glanced around the room. Josh and Raleigh were dancing several couples away, locked into each other's arms just like Tim and me. *Five, four, three, two, one . . .*

He saw me. Actually, Josh saw *us*. And he didn't look happy. I tilted my head upward and gazed once again into Tim's deep brown eyes. I inhaled, filling my lungs with air almost to the point of bursting. This was the moment. *One, two, three.* Exhale.

I clasped Tim's neck more firmly between my hands and pulled his head toward mine. "Go with me on this one," I whispered.

Tim nodded almost imperceptibly. A moment later we were kissing. Tim's lips were soft and warm, moving gently over mine. The rest of the party, the world, seemed to fall away as we pressed against each other, kissing, kissing, kissing. Tim's hands massaged my back, and I was dimly aware that my fingers had found their way into his thick dark hair.

From somewhere far away I remembered that the point of this kiss was not to enjoy myself. I was supposed to be making Josh jealous. I forced my eyes open. Josh had angrily torn himself from Raleigh's arms and was headed straight toward Tim and me.

I pulled my lips from Tim's and stepped out of his arms.

"Kiss this, Kaplan!" Josh shouted.

"What the—!" Tim exclaimed.

Josh's arm shot out from his side, then his fist connected with Tim's face.

I stared in horror as Tim crumpled to the floor, blood gushing from his nose.

"Josh, what are you *doing?*" I screamed.

"Ohmigod!" Maggie yelled, racing to Tim's side.

I knelt next to Tim and moved his head so that it was resting on my lap. This was getting *way* out of control. "Tim, are you all right?" I whispered.

"I think so. . . . I feel a little dizzy." His voice was low, and he was half slurring his words.

"Josh, are you insane?" Raleigh yelled from several feet away. "What's going on here?"

Josh looked from me to Raleigh. "I, uh . . . I don't know." He was breathing heavily, and his face was flushed.

C.J. and Danny stepped forward and grabbed Josh's arms. "Cool off, man," Danny said. "Pull yourself together."

"Use this to wipe up the blood." Raleigh held out a dish towel.

I took the towel and dabbed at the blood that ran from Tim's nose. "Uh, thanks." I was such a jerk. This was not going as I'd planned.

I glanced up and saw that Josh was staring at me. "Come on, Sara. We're leaving." He stepped away from C.J. and Danny and reached out his hand to me.

"Josh, I—"

"Now," he interrupted, his eyes stormy.

Raleigh frowned. "Josh, talk to me!" She looked as if she were about to cry. "I don't understand. . . ."

"I'm sorry, Raleigh," Josh said, his voice more gentle now. "But Sara and I have to leave."

An inner battle raged within me. Blood was still dripping from Tim's nose, and he didn't seem to be anywhere near ready to stand up. Half of me wanted to run out of the party with Josh, and the other half wanted to stay and take care of Tim. I mean, he'd taken a punch for me . . . but then again, Josh had *thrown* a punch for me. In all my years of dating and flirting I'd never had a guy do either one.

"Do you want to go with him, Sara?" Tim asked quietly. "Is that what you want?"

I gulped. "I . . . I . . ."

I felt Maggie's eyes on me, and I turned to her. "Mags, what do you think?" I whispered.

Her eyes answered my question. *Stay. Don't leave him here.* But aloud she simply said, "It's up to you."

Somewhere in the background I could hear Raleigh talking. She sounded upset, but I was too focused on the debate going on in my mind to clue in to exactly what she was saying. I just knew that this situation was getting worse and worse at a rapid rate. Was my staying at the party really going to help?

"Go ahead, Sara," Tim whispered finally. "I'll be fine."

I glanced at Maggie. "I can take over from here," she said, moving to the floor so that she could slip Tim's head into her lap. "I'll drive Tim's car home for him."

For what felt like an eternity, I stared at Tim's bleeding face. *Stay. Go. Stay. Go.*

"Sara, come on," Josh said gruffly. "Let's get out of here."

I rose from the floor—I'd waited too long for this moment to let it pass me by.

"Are you sure this is what you want to do?" Maggie asked quietly.

I nodded slowly. Then I threw Tim an apologetic glance and followed Josh out of the living room. As I walked away I felt Raleigh's eyes burning a hole in my back.

"Don't do this, Josh!" Raleigh called. "Don't walk away from me!"

But Josh kept going, and I kept following. With every step I waited for the sense of euphoria to overcome me. But as we continued down the hall and out the front door, I just felt horrible.

Josh had finally chosen me, and all I could think about was the blood running down Tim's face. I had won—but at what cost?

Twenty minutes later Josh and I pulled into the beach parking lot. From the front seat of his car I could see black waves crashing against the shore. I watched Josh throw the car into park, lost in thoughts of Tim.

Both Josh and I had been nearly silent during the drive over here. I didn't know what he was thinking, but I was consumed by images from the scene at the party. I could still hear Tim's voice gently telling me to leave with Josh. And I remembered the disappointment I'd seen in Maggie's face—I hadn't acted like the best friend she was accustomed to. I'd followed my heart and left my friends behind. I'd made a mistake, but there was nothing I could do to fix it now. The damage was done—at least until I could apologize.

Josh was gripping the steering wheel with both hands so tightly that even in the darkness I could see that his knuckles were white. Clearly it was time for a talk. I forced thoughts of Tim from my mind and cleared my throat. "Josh?" I said. "What happened tonight?"

He let go of the steering wheel and shifted in his seat so that we were facing each other. "I can't go on pretending with Raleigh anymore," Josh said. "I'll always love her, but I have to come to terms with the fact that I'm not *in* love with her anymore. Maybe I never was."

My heart leaped, my eyes watered, and goose bumps suddenly prickled my arms. Hearing these words come from Josh's mouth was almost surreal. I'd imagined this moment so many times that I almost couldn't believe it was happening.

"Do you really mean what you're saying?"

He nodded. "Yes." He leaned forward and switched off the car radio. "I'm going to break up with her tomorrow—if we're not already broken up anyway."

"Okay . . . good." I didn't know what else to say. I mean, it was the sort of moment when one expected oneself to rattle off some kind of prepared speech or something. But I had nothing to say . . . nothing.

"I love you, Sara." Josh put his arms around me and pulled me close.

At last I had him all to myself. As his head bent so that he could kiss my lips, I issued a silent thank-you to whoever or whatever ruled the universe. I'd finally gotten what I wanted.

"I've waited for this for so long," Josh whispered. "This is what's right—you and me, together forever."

Josh's gentle lips touched mine. I kissed him back,

putting my arms around his neck and slipping my fingers into his soft, blond hair. I waited for the heart-pounding excitement that I'd felt in Maine. I waited for the rush of love and affection. Instead I found myself comparing this kiss to Tim's. I remembered the way my spine had tingled when Tim had kissed me. I remembered the feel of Tim's hands around my waist, holding me close as we danced. What was my problem? I was seriously confused. *This moment is about you and Josh,* I told myself. *Forget Tim.*

Josh's lips moved from my mouth to my cheek to my ear, and the word *forever* echoed in my brain. Did I really want to be with Josh *forever?*

Josh pulled away and gazed into my eyes. "Tell me it's over between you and that dork. Tell me that from now on, you'll be mine and mine alone."

I didn't think now was the right time to point out that Tim was not a dork. Instead I smiled at Josh and traced his lips with my index finger. Obviously the only reason I was freaking out was because I couldn't really believe that this was happening. I *did* want to be with Josh forever—it's what I'd been dreaming about for months.

"Of course I'm yours," I whispered. "I've always been yours."

But as we kissed again, my mind was far away. I wasn't filled with that overpowering wave of love that I'd experienced during all those nights at camp.

I just need a little time to get used to all of this, I told myself. *In a few days everything will be perfect.*

★   ★   ★

I watched Josh's car drive down the street until the taillights disappeared into the night. I kept waiting for a rush of euphoria, but all I felt was deflated. Still, I was sure that my sadness had nothing to do with my feelings for Josh. It was just that I felt awful for having left Tim and Maggie at the party. I was ashamed of my behavior, and I knew that I had to find a way to make both of them understand how much I regretted my actions.

I would apologize to Maggie as soon as I got inside. If she forgave me, maybe I would then walk up the block to Tim's house. I could beg for his forgiveness tonight and not have this horrible guilt linger any longer.

I headed toward the front door, composing my apology in my head. As I neared the front porch I heard the faint sound of voices coming from the backyard.

I broke into a grin. I couldn't make out what they were saying, but there was no doubt that Tim and Maggie were sitting out on the dock. This was excellent—I could apologize to my two best friends, then go to sleep with a clear conscience. By morning I would have settled into the new status of my relationship with Josh and I would be happy, happy, happy.

I practically skipped through the yard as I made my way toward the dock. Tonight was going to turn out all right after all.

I stopped in my tracks as the dock came into view. Maggie and Tim were there—but they weren't talking. My two best friends were *hugging*— in a very intimate way. Suddenly I remembered the way they'd flirted with each other that afternoon and that pang of jealousy returned, but this time it felt a million times stronger.

I thought of the way Tim had kissed me tonight. Had he been kissing Maggie the same way? For reasons I couldn't begin to fathom, the idea made me crazy.

I stood frozen. I felt as if Mike Tyson had just punched me in the stomach. I couldn't breathe, and there were tiny black dots floating in front of my eyes. Still, I could see that Tim was touching Maggie's face—just as he had touched mine when we danced.

"What are you *doing?*" I yelled. I hadn't realized that the words were coming from my mouth until they were already speeding through the air and landing on Tim's and Maggie's ears.

I yanked myself out of my temporary paralysis and stomped over to the deck. "What are you doing?" I repeated stupidly. I mean, it was obvious what they were doing. They were making out.

"Oh, Sara, hi," Maggie said, clearly startled. "We didn't expect you to come home so early. . . ."

"How's lover boy?" Tim asked. His eyes were dark, and his voice sounded more distant than I'd ever heard it before. He sounded as if he were talking to a stranger.

I was filled with inexplicable rage, the force of which was making me dizzy. "I can't believe I actually felt bad about leaving you at the party!" I told them.

"Sara, what—" Tim stood up and took a step toward me.

"Never mind. Just go back to what you were doing," I choked out. "I was going to apologize, but I can see that you're both doing fine without me."

"Are you okay? What's going on?" Maggie asked.

"I . . . I—" There were no words to articulate what was going on in my head. I didn't *know* what was going on in my head. I just knew that I wanted to get away from Tim and Maggie as soon as humanly possible. Rather than answer Maggie's question, I turned and fled, jealousy, anger, and sadness tearing away at me.

Sara's Recipe for Disaster

For anyone who wants to have the worst night in the history of their entire life, this zesty dish will please your palette. Unfortunately I'm speaking from experience.

Ingredients:

1 concerned best friend in from out of town
1 great guy who you think of as a friend
1 cute but ultimately limited jock who you think you're in love with
1 girlfriend of cute but ultimately limited jock
1 short white dress
1 pair matching sandals

Directions:

Apply dress and sandals to your person. Then bring together your best friend, the girlfriend, and the two guys, preferably at a crowded party where any unpleasantness will do the maximum amount of damage to the ego of anyone involved. Once the room reaches a high temperature, make the scene of your choice. Finally flee the party and wait for the chips to fall. I guarantee, you won't be disappointed.

Thirteen

I'D BEEN LYING awake in bed for over an hour, but I was no closer to sleep. I'd counted sheep, I'd recited the alphabet sixty times, I'd gone over every detail of my time with Josh. But I was still wide-awake. And being conscious at this moment was nothing short of torture.

The one subject I didn't want to ponder, my anger at Tim and Maggie, was the one subject that wouldn't let itself slide from my brain. I was helpless. It was 1:03 A.M. when I heard the back door open softly and then close.

I listened as Maggie tiptoed up the creaky staircase. A moment later she paused in front of my bedroom door. There was a quiet tap, tap, tap. "Sara?" she whispered. "Are you awake?" The door opened several inches.

I shut my eyes quickly and forced my face muscles to relax. I couldn't face Maggie now. I didn't know what I would say—I still hadn't come to terms with why I'd reacted so strongly out there on the dock. I hadn't *let* myself figure it out.

"I just want you to know that there's nothing going on between Tim and me," Maggie said softly. "All you saw was a friendly hug. But we'll talk about it tomorrow. Try to get some sleep. And remember: best friends forever." With that she closed my bedroom door and quietly walked down the hall toward the guest room.

I opened my eyes and stared at the ceiling, silently thanking Maggie for being such an amazing friend. She always knew exactly what I needed to hear. I replayed her words in my mind, tears springing to my eyes and overflowing onto my cheeks. I felt an overwhelming combination of relief and anguish as tear after tear slid down my face. *There's nothing going on between Tim and me.* Why did that sentence mean everything to me—even more than Josh telling me that he loved me?

I played a mental movie of the last few months of my life. I saw myself bright and smiling in Maine: There were fireside kisses with Josh and long romantic walks along the lake. I remembered Josh's compliments—I'd loved each and every one of them. But I realized now that Josh and I had never really communicated. Josh didn't know *me*.

Then I thought of Tim. I thought of the way he'd looked at me when he'd sculpted my face. Tim knew I was afraid of sharks. He knew that more than anything I wanted both of my parents to find a person they could share their lives with. Tim understood the hills and valleys of my moods. And I understood him. I recognized the look in his eye when he had an idea for a new piece of art. I could hear the subtle impatience in his voice when he tried to explain the concept of invoices to my dad.

Finally I thought of Tim's kiss. It had been a perfect moment in time . . . until I'd destroyed it. What if the kiss had gone on . . . and on and on? Nothing sounded more wonderful, more enticing.

And then I realized that I'd known the truth for a long time now. I wasn't in love with Josh—maybe I never had been. But I *was* in love. I was madly, passionately, head over heels in love with the greatest guy I'd ever known. I was in love with Tim.

How could I have been so unbearably stupid? Tim was the guy who made me laugh. He was the guy who had proved time and time again that he was worthy of my respect, my admiration, my trust. Tim had been there for me since the first day I met him.

Oh, Tim, why didn't I see that you were the one? I asked myself. I had pursued Josh like a demon, and in the process I'd shown Tim the absolute worst aspects of my personality. Just thinking of the things I'd asked him to do in the name of my obsession made me cringe.

There was no way I could hope to win Tim's love now. I'd let him down when he needed me, and then I'd acted like a complete freak on the dock. I hadn't even given him a much deserved apology. How could he ever forgive me, much less love me?

I didn't try to stop the tears that coursed down my cheeks. Why should I? I'd blown any chance I might have had to win Tim's love by acting like a selfish, spoiled brat. There was no way he would fall in love with me now . . . was there?

But then I thought about the fact that even through all my crazy behavior, Tim had stood by me. He'd always forgiven me. Was it possible that he felt the same way about me that I felt about him? I couldn't stop the tiny flicker of hope that began within my heart. Maybe, just maybe, it wasn't too late for Tim and me.

I was operating on approximately forty-five minutes of sleep when I rang the Nelsons' doorbell early Saturday morning. Thank goodness I was prepared for the sounds of "When the Saints Go Marching In"—I couldn't have taken more surprises than were absolutely necessary.

At seven that morning I had dragged myself out of bed and written Maggie a note of apology. I slid the note under her door, where she would find it when she awoke (probably sometime around noon). Then I'd taken off on a mission to set my world right again. Talking to Josh was phase one.

Josh answered the front door. He didn't look much better than I felt. His eyes were red, and his hair was an unbrushed mess. Apparently he hadn't gotten much sleep last night either.

"We made a mistake," I said quickly. "You saw Tim kissing me, and you were jealous."

"Sara, I—"

I held up one hand. "Let me finish." I took a deep breath. "We had a great time last summer, but . . ." Man, I felt terrible. Josh had finally fallen hard for me, and I was about to break his heart.

"Yeah, it was a great summer—"

"But I think we got carried away . . . and, and . . . I'm in love with someone else." I paused. "I'm in love with Tim."

It was the first time I'd said the words aloud. My head felt as if it were going to explode. Literally. I wouldn't have been at all surprised if brain matter oozed out of my ears and splattered onto the Nelsons' front steps. I loved Tim. I *loved* him. Oh, man, this was huge. It was, like, the biggest thing that had ever happened to me.

"Sara, can I say something?" Josh asked.

I hoped he wasn't going to beg. I felt guilty enough already. "Of course."

Josh ran a hand through his shaggy blond hair, a gesture that I had once found endearing but that now just made me nervous. "I agree with you."

My eyes widened. "What?"

"You're absolutely right. I've been up all night, thinking. Sometime before sunrise I realized that this whole thing between us was crazy. I mean, we don't even know each other all that well."

"Oh." I smiled. I don't know why, but for some reason this conversation was suddenly making me want to burst out in hysterical giggles. "Well, then."

"I'm glad you feel the same way—I didn't want to hurt you." Josh leaned forward and kissed me softly on the forehead. "You're a great girl, but you're not the one for me."

"So . . . uh, are you going to get back together with Raleigh?" I asked. Shockingly enough, I hoped his answer would be yes.

"Well, we never officially broke up," Josh said. "I haven't even talked to her since the party last night. . . . She probably hates me."

Josh's voice was heavy with despair and heartbreak. I recognized the tone immediately—it was exactly how I'd sounded on the phone with Maggie when I'd found out that Josh already had a girlfriend. Finally the whole picture of what had been going on for the last few weeks emerged from the murky depths of my self-deluded mind.

Josh *was* in love with Raleigh. Josh had always been in love with Raleigh. Yes, he had liked me. He'd been attracted to me. I was fairly sure that there had been moments in Maine last summer when he'd even fancied himself in love with me. But I was merely a distraction—an aggressive distraction. Josh never would have written me that promised letter. If I hadn't been playing with his mind for the last couple of weeks, he never would have doubted that Raleigh was the one he really wanted to be with.

"She'll forgive you," I told him.

There were actual tears in his eyes as he looked

168

at me. "Do you really think so? Why? How?"

I laughed. Who would have believed that the day would arrive when I was dispensing romantic advice to Josh Nelson? Life truly was absurd. In some way I felt as if this whole crazy ride had been a journey into my heart. I just hoped that I would find Tim waiting for me at the final destination.

"Because she loves you."

"I hope so. Well, I guess I'll see you around," Josh said softly.

"I guess so."

I turned and headed down the brick path. Just like the last time I'd walked from the front steps of Josh's house to my car, my heart was pounding. But now those painful thumps had nothing to do with Josh. My heart was racing because I now knew who my true love was . . . and I was going to find him.

Tim's beat-up old van was in the beach parking lot, just as I had hoped. I was grateful that he'd mentioned yesterday afternoon that he was going to go on a morning dive. It was still so early, there were only a few cars parked in the lot. I'd been in Florida long enough to know that all the vehicles probably belonged to fishermen and hopeful surfers.

I slammed on the brakes of my Oldsmobile and threw the car into park. Now that I knew Tim was close by, I didn't feel as if I could wait one more second to spill my guts to him. I didn't care if he spat in my face and told me he never wanted to speak to me again. I *had* to tell him how I felt.

My thongs slapped against the sand as I raced toward the water. *Be there,* I prayed. *Please, please, be on the shore.*

And then I saw him. Tim was in his wet suit, concentrating on strapping a tank of air to his back. I'd never seen a more beautiful sight. Had there really been a time when I'd blown off a scuba-diving lesson with Tim to hang out with Josh? It just didn't seem possible.

"Tim!" I yelled. "Tim!"

He dropped the tank. "Sara."

I jogged toward him, getting closer and closer. Close enough to see that his cheeks were pale and his nose was red from where Josh had punched him. Tim looked almost as bad as Josh had—which for some perverse reason I took as a good omen. Hey, desperate girls will cling to *anything.*

"Can we talk?" I asked. "I promise, no more yelling."

Tim sank gracefully to the sand and looked at me expectantly. "I'm listening."

I sat down beside him, my heart beating a thousand times a minute. "I've been a fool . . . an idiot. . . ."

Tim grinned. "So far I agree with everything you're saying."

Okay, I deserved that. "I don't love Josh," I said. "I don't think I ever did. You were right—I just didn't want to lose."

He nodded. "I'm glad you realized that." He stood up again. "Now, if there isn't anything else, I'd like to go scuba diving."

I scrambled to my feet. He obviously didn't feel the same way about me that I felt about him. But I still had to say the words—they were burning a hole in my brain. "But I am in love, Tim."

He froze in place. "You are?"

I nodded, trying to memorize the shape and size of each gold fleck that sparkled in his chocolate brown eyes. "I'm in love with you."

For a long moment Tim didn't say anything. He looked out at the Atlantic, then up toward the parking lot, then, finally, back at me. "You really hurt me last night, Sara."

"I know." How could I explain that the girl who had walked out of the party hadn't really been me? She had been some evil alter ego who I'd killed and buried late last night. "I'm so sorry. I'll never forgive myself for abandoning you like that."

"I got a punch in the nose, and you got a romantic evening with the guy of your dreams."

"But it wasn't romantic," I told him. "The whole time I was with Josh, all I could think about was you."

I could see his entire face soften. "Really?"

I nodded. "I thought about what a jerk I'd been, and I thought about the way you kissed me." I was whispering now. "I think I realized the moment I left the party that Josh wasn't the one for me and you were."

"You're sure about this?"

"I've never been so sure of anything in my life."

Finally Tim glanced up at the sky. "Thank

you," he whispered. Tim stepped forward and slipped his arms around my shoulders. He pulled me close and hugged me against his tall, lean body. "You don't know how long I've waited to hear you say those words."

I smiled wider than I'd ever smiled before. I'd never been as happy as I was at that moment as I felt myself melting into his embrace. We just stood there, silently hugging, enjoying each other's warmth.

Then I pulled away a bit and looked up at Tim. "I'm sorry that I freaked out on you and Maggie last night. I guess I was crazy jealous."

Tim laughed. "Poor Maggie—she had to listen to me go on and on about you forever." He squeezed my arms and dropped a light kiss on my forehead. "Watching you leave that party with Josh killed me. I just couldn't hold my feelings inside anymore."

"Wow." This was too good to be true.

He placed one finger under my chin and leaned forward so that our foreheads were touching. "I told Maggie everything. I told her how I'd been in love with you since the first day we met. I told her that I'd considered hiring a hit man to take out Josh while you weren't looking. I told her that more than anything, I wanted you to fall in love with me."

"Wow," I whispered again.

Our lips met as if we had kissed a thousand times. Life was beginning anew, and this time I was going to do everything right. Tingles emanated from every nerve in my body, and my head felt as if it had become unattached from my body and floated away. There was Tim, and there was me. Nothing and no one else existed.

When Tim pulled away, only the strength of his arms kept me from melting into a puddle on the sand. He touched his forehead again to mine. "We're going to have to take this slow," Tim said. "I want us to start from the beginning."

"I want that too," I assured him.

"And this time everything between us is going to be real—no lies, no games, no make-believe."

I nodded. "No games. Just promise me that you're going to stick around for a while."

"I will *definitely* be sticking around."

My smile was so wide, I felt as if my face were going to break into two pieces.

He smiled back at me. "Now, can I interest you in another scuba-diving lesson?"

"I'd love to, but right now I have to be somewhere. I owe my best friend the greatest brunch she's ever had."

Tim hugged me tight one more time, then released me. "Go hang with Maggie. I'll see you later."

What wonderful words. *I'll see you later.*

I turned and jogged back toward my car, feeling more as if I were walking on water than trudging through sand. And as soon as I told Maggie how sorry I was, life would be perfect.

Sara's Gratitude Journal
—which she is now keeping
faithfully (thanks, Oprah)

    I am grateful for Tim—so grateful that I could fill up a whole journal just writing that over and over again.

    I am grateful that my dad finally asked a woman out on a date—her name is Tina, and she's a printmaker— and I like her!

    I am grateful that Mom is having a wonderful time in Tokyo.

    I am grateful that Maggie is going to come to Florida during winter break (with Matt) for a whole week!

    I am grateful that I have grown up—that I am now as worried about inner beauty as I am about outer beauty, winning, and all of those other things.

    I am grateful for Tim. Did I say that already?

Epilogue

I WALKED LIGHTLY on the ocean floor, mesmerized by the richness of life below the sea. Thank goodness I'd finally gotten those scuba-diving lessons from Tim. Now that I was certified, I was the one begging Tim every weekend to explore the bottom of the ocean with me.

A few feet away Tim moved easily through the water. Even in his scuba-diving gear, he was beautiful. Memories of our kisses last night and the half-hour-long food fight we'd had in the backyard flooded my mind. I was still dazzled by the gift Tim had given me a couple of days ago. I'd placed the small sculpture of my face in a position of prominence in my room. I wanted it to be the first thing I saw in the morning and the last thing I saw before I went to bed.

I broke out of my musings as Tim motioned toward me. And then my heart stopped, or sped up. I was too terrified to determine which reaction I was having. There, beside Tim, was a small shark. My worst nightmare was coming true! I was trapped dozens of feet below the surface of the water with a shark mere feet away from me.

I watched in amazement as Tim reached out and touched the side of the shark. For a moment I closed my eyes in terror, positive that he was going to be eaten alive. For that matter, I was positive that we were *both* going to be eaten alive. But when I forced myself to pry open my eyelids, I saw that Tim was grinning behind his mask. The shark was still swimming lazy circles around him, and Tim was motioning me forward.

Oh, no. He wanted *me* to touch the thing. Tim drifted closer and clasped my hand. Gently he guided me forward. I took a deep breath from my tank of air. If Tim thought that it was safe to touch the shark, then it had to be all right.

With my free hand I reached out and touched the shark's back. It felt smooth and cold and oddly beautiful. As I moved away my fingers in amazement the shark swam one more circle, then headed out into the ocean.

Behind his mask Tim's dark brown eyes were beaming at me. "I love you," he mouthed.

"I love you," I mouthed back.

I think it was at that moment that I truly understood all that being in love meant. Love was trust and growing and safety. Tim and I had all of those things, and they were growing stronger every day.

In the depths of the sea Tim tightened his grip on my hand and pulled me close. When we hugged, I felt that my heart would overflow with happiness. This, after all, was the real thing. I had reached the last stop on my journey into my heart . . . and somehow I had been lucky enough to find paradise.

Do you ever wonder about falling in love? About members of the opposite sex? Do you need a little friendly advice but have no one to turn to? Well, that's where we come in . . . Jenny and Jake. Send us those questions you're dying to ask, and we'll give you the straight scoop on life and love.

DEAR JAKE

Q: *I love spending time with my boyfriend, and I also love hanging out with my friends. I just wish I could do both at once, but my boyfriend never wants us to go places together. Why are guys so weird about getting to know their girlfriends' friends?*

LP, Austin, TX

A: Okay, how appealing does this sound to you: You're in your boyfriend's basement with him and the guys, listening to them tell jokes about bodily functions and exchange news about the girls they're after. Did you really need to know that Jane looks better when she wears those tight shirts? I'm guessing no.

The logic works both ways—I don't feel the need to know which nail polish stays on longest without chipping, one of the things I learned when I accompanied my girlfriend and her friends to the mall once. Essentially we feel uncomfortable around you and your girlfriends because we don't relate to a lot of what you discuss with one another. On a one-on-one basis, we like to meet and get to know the people who are important to you, but on these group outings we're outnumbered and unsure of how to act. I'm sure your boyfriend will respond well if you encourage him to talk to your friends individually and in more casual situations. But for your nights on the town, try to understand that he doesn't want to intrude on the girl bonding.

Q: *I know it's supposed to be guys who pressure girls to move fast, but my boyfriend is the total opposite. At first I thought it was great that he was so sensitive, but now I'm wondering if there's something wrong with me. He won't even kiss me that much—he just gives me light pecks on the lips. Are any other guys like this, and why?*

LS, Frederick, MD

A: First of all, I'm sure that there is absolutely nothing wrong with you. And yes, plenty of other guys are shy like your boyfriend. As much as he is probably dying to kiss you, his insecurities are most likely keeping him frozen in fear. His thoughts when you're close: *Does she want me to kiss her? How exactly do I do this? Am I a good kisser? Will she get mad at me if I do it wrong or don't know when I should stop?*

Your role here is to reassure him that everything is cool with you and you're ready to get closer. Maybe you need to make the first move or even admit that you're a little nervous and ask if he is too. Laugh at the awkwardness of the moment until both of you are comfortable enough to enjoy each other and have fun, which is what this is all supposed to be about anyway.

DEAR JENNY

Q: *I overheard some guys talking about the kind of girls they like, and I don't fit the description at all. What does this mean?*

PW, Grenada, MS

A: What it means is that you probably won't ever go out with those guys. Actually it doesn't even mean that—try making a list of everything you want in a guy, and then compare the list to the guys you've dated. Notice any differences? I read many letters from girls who want to know how they should change to win the guys of their dreams, and the answer I give is always the same—don't. If you try to be someone you're not, you'll never be happy with yourself or with the guy who's with you for false reasons. There is definitely someone out there who has always been looking for everything that you are, and don't give up until you find him.

Q: *My friend Alicia has liked this guy Raphael for a long time, but he doesn't know. Recently he asked me out, and I didn't know what to do because I would have said yes if it weren't for Alicia. I said no, but now I don't know if I should tell her that he asked me out or not.*

DB, Tucson, AZ

A: It was very loyal of you to turn down a guy who you're also interested in to avoid hurting your friend. And your concern about telling her what happened is more proof of how much you care about Alicia. But you might just have to hurt her a little to really do the right thing. Alicia needs to know the truth about this guy if she's been harboring feelings for him for a long time and he doesn't share the sentiment. It's not fair to keep her in the dark, and if she finds it out through anyone but you, she'll feel betrayed and also wonder why you didn't want to tell her and what *else* you might be hiding. Be supportive because she'll need it. Hearing that your crush likes your friend is pretty tough news to swallow. She'll get over it with time, though, and she'll be grateful for what a good friend she has in you.

Do you have questions about love? Write to:
Jenny Burgess or Jake Korman
c/o Daniel Weiss Associates
33 West 17th Street
New York, NY 10011

Don't miss any of the books in *Love Stories*
—the romantic series from Bantam Books!

Real life. Real friends. Real faith.

Clearwater Crossing—where
friendships are formed, hearts
come together, choices have
consequences, and lives
are changed
forever . . .

#1

#2

#3

#4

clearwater crossing

**An inspirational new series
available now wherever books are sold.**

You'll always remember your first love.

Love Stories

Looking for signs he's ready to fall in love?

Want the guy's point of view?

Then you should check out *Love Stories*. Romantic stories that tell it like it is—why he doesn't call, how to ask him out, when to say good-bye.

Love Stories

Available wherever books are sold.